Best Served Cold

Michael R. Davidson
17 Lillards Road
New Market, VA 22844-3705

Library of Congress Control Number: 2024910970
Print ISBN: 979-8-218-43308-6
eBook ISBN: 979-8-218-43361-1

Contact author at info@michaelrdavidson.com

Cover by

Printed and Bound in the United States of America

First Edition

Also by Michael R. Davidson

Harry's Rules

Eye for an Eye

Incubus

The Incubus Vendetta

The Inquisitor and the Maiden
(Caliphate Book I)

Retribution
(Caliphate Book II)

Krystal

The Dead Lawyer

Spilled Blood

The Dove

A Peculiar Profession

Buy Another Day

With Kseniya Kirillova

In the Shadow of Mordor

Successor

This novel is dedicated to my buddies and colleagues in the "Old Hands Group." Old spies just fade away into the swirling mist.

BEST SERVED COLD

A Krystal Murphy Mystery

By

Michael R. Davidson

Best Served Cold

Some memories fade with time, but this one persisted in its horrible clarity as if etched into stone.

With no little exertion, he heaved the body into the trunk of the dead man's car. The body was heavy. A few moments earlier, he had wrapped the corpse's bloody head in clear plastic and then covered it with a towel.

A woman stood beside the car, hugging herself and weeping. He closed the trunk lid and stepped to her, embraced her, and whispered assurances into her ear. He did not want to leave her, but time was of the essence. His journey would be long, and he had to reach his destination before dawn.

He opened the car door and glanced up at the house before getting in. In an upstairs bedroom window, he saw the face of the boy, his eyes saucers and his mouth forming an "O." Something would have to be done about the boy, but that was a problem for later. Disposal of the body in the trunk was the first task.

Yes, the boy was a problem. He would think about it as he drove. Scandal must be avoided, especially for the frail woman who was so dear to him. The rear-view mirror revealed her still standing in front of the house as he drove away.

He was wrong. In the end, scandal was as inevitable as the rising of the sun.

It was just after 10 P.M., which would give him just enough time. He had checked the car's fuel gauge and found that the tank was nearly full.

He eased the Mercedes onto the street and headed for Interstate 85. The drive from Charlotte to Nags Head would take close to six hours, and he would have to drive carefully, keeping to the speed limit. He could not afford to be stopped by the police.

It was early morning, just after 4:30 A.M. when he pulled to a stop at the Thicket Lump Marina at the southern tip of Nags Head. As expected, the place was deserted at that hour. He turned off the Mercedes' lights and coasted to a stop at the slip where he kept his Hanover 525 motor yacht. As quickly as he could, he transferred the body to the boat and dragged it to the lower deck where he covered it with a tarpaulin. Hoping against hope that he had been unobserved, he drove away from the marina and crossed back over the Virginia Dare Memorial Bridge heading back west. The fuel gauge light was blinking which meant he would have to chance stopping to refill the tank.

He pulled off the highway to an all-night gas station. He would have to go inside to pay in cash.

Dawn was coming, and the next part of his plan was equally risky and depended more on luck than careful planning.

Best Served Cold

CHAPTER 1

"Hi. My name is Krystal Murphy, and I'm an alcoholic."

The well-worn words drummed a tattoo into her skull, and she didn't like the rhythm. Krystal Murphy did not like admitting to a weakness of any sort, and the more she thought about it, the less likely it seemed that she would ever utter those words.

Her friends had put her in touch with a member of Alcoholics Anonymous. Much against her better instincts but submitting nonetheless to her friends' encouragement, Krystal had agreed to the meeting at a sushi bar in Charlotte's upscale Southpark Shopping Mall where she was met by a zaftig, middle-aged lady who dripped with sympathy and whose eyes betrayed a sad past.

Krystal prided herself on her independence and strength of character which her father long ago had described as "mule headed." Maybe, but she always got results. She'd served as an Army MP in some difficult places, including war zones. Moving from the military to a job with the

Arlington, Virginia police, she had earned more than her share of glory, a fact which had served to arouse resentment in certain types of male cops she had to work with, especially when she had been promoted over others to head the department's robbery-homicide squad.

One particularly difficult and bloody case had taken her to Miami where she met with a charming Cuban American cop named Ray Velasquez and sooner than she would have expected she found herself in the sack with him. He was charming, funny, intelligent, and beguiled her with Latin charm in the tropical heat of Miami. The city was exotic to her, far from the cornfields of her Hoosier childhood and the hectic atmosphere of the Washington, DC suburbs. He introduced her to mojitos, sweet Cuban coffee, and love in the warm, tropical afternoon. She found contentment and joy in his arms and thought it would never end.

She now chided herself for such girlish foolishness.

The affair had ended when she accepted an offer from former CIA operative Robert Strachey to join his new private security and investigative firm in Charlotte, North Carolina. The long-distance relationship with Velasquez was already strained to the breaking point. He wanted her with him in Miami, but she could not oblige. Despite her strength and fortitude, the end of the only serious long-term relationship she had ever experienced left her feeling alone and helpless against her worst instincts. She dove headfirst into a bottle of scotch, and her behavior dismayed and alarmed her friends.

She had always been able to drink, in college, through her Army years, and her time with the Arlington Police. But the loss of that man had broken the barrier between social drinking and dependence on alcohol for surcease. What was worse, the break-up had been entirely of her own making. She had chosen her work over everything else, had been incapable of compromise, "mule headed," and it had driven the man away. She had hit bottom but was fortunate to have friends who cared. Bob and Amy Strachey had picked her up off the floor and pointed her toward AA. If for nothing more than gratitude she had reluctantly agreed to have a chat with a representative of the organization.

She gritted her teeth, unable to dispel the image of herself serving donuts and coffee at AA meetings and, worst of all, standing in front of a group of strangers and declaring that she was an alcoholic. She didn't believe she was an alcoholic.

She was fully aware of the dangers of overdrinking - liver damage, pancreatitis, decline into dependency and eventual ruin. Her retreat into the bottle had not been due to any overwhelming desire for alcohol; it had been a temporary escape from a serious personal problem and its resulting despair, and not a little self-loathing. But there remained the nagging thought that her chosen means of escape might also suggest a tendency to dependency on an alcoholic crutch. She consciously shunned the idea and had shunned drink, at least for a while, to test herself. She didn't think she needed AA.

Krystal saw AA as a crutch, a support group to lean on while rebuilding self-esteem. The zaftig woman insisted it was much more than that, explaining that the organization relied on a higher power. God had not been a part of Krystal's life since childhood, and her years as a police officer had soured her view of humanity to the point where she could see no chance of redemption for herself or anyone else.

The organization's other major challenge went against the grain of her personality. She had always seen herself as strong and persistent, but she learned that the first rule of AA, the first "Step" of the famous12 Steps was the requirement to admit defeat. Pride and self-confidence did not figure in the equation. According to AA, alcoholics are the victims of a mental obsession so powerful that it could not be overcome by willpower alone.

The AA representative did not try to push. Scare tactics were seldom productive. Proselytizing was more successful if done gently.

Krystal had never in her life thought of herself as helpless or a victim, and rather than enticing her to join AA, the conversation served only to bolster her insistence on self-reliance.

In one of the organization's brochures, there was a passage that caught her eye: "only problem drinkers themselves, individually, can determine whether or not they are in fact alcoholics."

OK, she thought, drinking had recently become a problem, but a problem did not necessarily indicate a disease.

CHAPTER 2

According to the morning paper, a 2.2 earthquake had been registered in Buncombe County shortly after midnight. That was about 130 miles from Charlotte, and neither Krystal nor anyone else in Charlotte had felt anything. Strange that the ancient mountains of the Eastern U.S. should still display such tectonic activity, like an old person rolling over in bed. She wondered idly if there had been any earthquakes in Northern Virginia while she was there, other than the political ones.

She had feared the move from Arlington to Charlotte would be traumatic. Colleagues at the Arlington Police Department thought she had taken leave of her senses. It was complicated. She did not suffer fools lightly, and was convinced that Northern Virginia and Washington, D.C. offered ample proof that the Peter Principle was alive and well. Arlington was a bedroom community of Washington, and Northern Virginia was rife with Federal Government installations, including the CIA, only a few miles from Arlington on the George Washington Memorial Parkway. She had become entangled in some cases that involved the CIA as well as the FBI. Those experiences had enhanced her Arlington Police career, but they had revealed some dark truths she would just as soon forget.

She was amused when locals complained about the traffic in Charlotte, which they sometimes referred to as "carlot." Compared to the permanent traffic jam in the DC area, this was a walk in the park, and the pleasant early spring weather was a bonus this morning. The month of May had tiptoed into Charlotte gently with a welcome warming in the air with drew the sap up the trees to create new foliage to shade the broad avenues of the Queen City.

Fifteen minutes after driving out of her apartment parking lot, she entered the gleaming white marble lobby at 300 South Tryon Street and took an elevator to the 21st floor where she pushed through the oak double doors into Robert Strachey's world.

Somewhere along the way Strachey had developed a fondness for the decorating style one finds in the men's clubs along London's Pall Mall. As a result, the office boasted specially installed plank floors, antique Persian rugs, and overstuffed leather furniture. It was decidedly male, and she didn't mind it, at all.

She was greeted by a pleasant middle-aged lady behind an impressive, mahogany trimmed reception desk set before a green marble wall with the firm's name in big, brass letters: PRIVATE SECURITY AND INQUIRIES. The lady's name was Ruth Scatterfield, and she was the receptionist and mother hen of the office. For a reason known only to her, Ruth recently had dyed her hair pink which somehow did not clash with her lime green pant suit. She greeted Krystal with a bright smile and a honey-accented greeting. "Hello, darlin'."

"There's someone here to see you," she continued, nodding toward the row of chairs set against the wall on the right where a man sat nervously tapping his feet.

"He asked specifically for you," finished Ruth.

Krystal introduced herself, and he stood and said his name was Lawrence Terrell. His handshake was limp and as cold as a dead frog in her firm grip. He followed her down the plushily carpeted corridor to her office and took a seat in a chair facing her desk. He was tall, lanky, and twitchy, with black hair that hung in his eyes. His weathered features and rough hands, the grime around his fingernails which seemed permanently embedded suggested his age at somewhere over thirty. She had known people like this, people who had lived rough and hard. He wore new jeans and a cotton pullover, and his feet were encased in a pair of expensive Nikes. Every item of clothing looked brand new. Unless he had benefited from an extensive shoplifting spree at Neiman Marcus, he was not living on the streets. It was his eyes that held her attention. They were old eyes, suspicious eyes with a feral gleam.

The combination of those eyes and his tense body language put Krystal instantly on guard. This type of person could be a coiled spring ready to release with destructive energy. "May I see some identification, Mr. Terrell? It's a standard request we make of all prospective clients. We need to know with whom we are dealing."

"But I just told you who I am," he said, his old eyes squinting to slits.

She continued in a calm voice. "Yes, but we are required to confirm the identity of clients. We ask the same of everybody."

Of course, they did not. But Terrell made her uneasy.

After a pause, he pulled a wallet from his back pocket and produced a Tennessee driver's license, which he handed over with a scowl.

"Very well," said Krystal as she returned the license. She was surprised to see that Terrell was only 25.

She asked, "What brings you to our office?"

"My name means nothing to you?"

"Should it?"

"You're not from Charlotte, are you?" he said, his eyes not wavering from her.

"No. I've only been here a little over a year and a half."

He smiled thinly and nodded and murmured to himself, "That might be a good thing."

"Does it make any difference that I'm not from here?" she asked.

"If you knew this town, you would recognize the name," he said. "But maybe it's for the best. You can be more objective."

"Why don't you just tell me why you're here?"

"My family is well-known here," he began. "But I haven't seen them in a long time. I just returned to Charlotte a little over a week ago, and I scared the shit out of them." He gave her a sly look. "I had to wait, you see, until I had the means to be independent." He paused again and grew silent in introspection. After a beat, he continued, "My father, James Terrell, disappeared when I was a boy, but I know he was murdered."

His face assumed a defiant look, as if he didn't expect her to believe him.

The words tumbled out of him now. "It was my uncle Randolph, I know. I saw him load my father's body into a car. I was very young, and a lot of things are fuzzy, but I know what I saw."

"Didn't the police investigate?"

"I suppose they did. But they didn't find anything. No one asked me a damned thing."

"Why would your uncle want to kill your father?"

"He and my mother were having an affair. They got married and now control both the family businesses. They are very rich."

"This happened a long time ago, Mr. Terrell, when you were a child. Are you certain the police found nothing? Surely, they must have had their suspicions. There must have been an investigation."

Lawrence lowered his head. "I was young at the time, yes. And no one told me anything." He suddenly jerked upright, startling her. "But my uncle moved into the house, and now they're married."

"That must have been very traumatic for you," said Krystal.

"They sent me away to school almost immediately. They knew what I suspected and didn't want to have me around."

"A lot of time has passed, Mr. Terrell. It would be exceedingly difficult to uncover anything new. Are you sure you want to do this? It would be quite expensive."

Terrell gave her a lopsided smile, revealing stained teeth. "Don't worry about money," he said. "I have plenty of it now. After my 25th birthday I was able to access the trust fund my father set up for me. That was just a week ago. There was nothing my mother or uncle could do to prevent it. They're not happy I came back. Won't even let me stay at the house – my house. I had to move into a hotel."

All sorts of people came to the office soliciting their services, but Lawrence Terrell was unique in a way which was hard to categorize. And he didn't look like the sort of person able to afford the firm's fees despite his claim to wealth.

"I'll tell you what," she said, temporizing. "Let me look into the matter for a couple of days before deciding whether to take the case. Will that be OK?"

Terrell nodded slowly, clearly dissatisfied with her response. "I came to you first because this firm has a good reputation. I read about how you solved the Nessmith murders last year. But there are other detective agencies in town that will be glad to take my money, and I can always go to them."

"That would be your prerogative, Mr. Terrell," she hoped he would look elsewhere, "but I can't accept a case blindly. I need to check the facts before I can give you an answer. And we will require a retainer until there is a decision. You'll get it back if we don't accept the case."

Terrell frowned, but he said, "OK, I'll be back in three days."

He pulled what looked like a brand-new checkbook from his rear pocket and wrote out a check in the requested amount. He laid the check on her desk and stalked out of the office without another word.

First things first. She walked down the hallway to the IT shop and initiated background checks on Lawrence Terrell, James Terrell, and the rest of the family. The Internet, she had discovered, saved a lot of shoe leather, and it could reach more deeply into people's lives than they could ever imagine.

Then she phoned Sergeant Archie Wolf of the Charlotte Mecklenburg Police Department. Archie was Chief of Staff and all-around go-to guy for Captain Abel Curry, the occasionally cantankerous chief of the Homicide/ADW Unit. Archie was a deceptively clever, unrepentant North Carolina redneck who drove a beat-up Jeep Wrangler with knobby oversized tires and was the kind of shot with any sort of weapon that would make Daniel Boone proud. His skill had saved Krystal's life a year earlier. She was no city-slicker herself having been raised in rural southern Indiana amidst square miles of pancake flat corn and milo fields, which engendered the easygoing friendship which had grown between the two.

CHAPTER 3

Charlotte Mecklenburg Police Headquarters is located at Government Plaza at the opposite end of the city center from the PSI offices. Archie Wolf had responded immediately to her request for a meeting, and she was there ten minutes later. As a former cop Krystal still responded to the atmosphere whenever she entered a police precinct with its uniformed occupants busy at their assigned duties. The familiar sounds and smells struck a chord with her.

After over a year and a half in Charlotte everyone in the building knew her, knew she was an ex-cop, and accepted her. She waved at the desk sergeant and took the elevator to the third floor and was soon knocking on the door to Archie's office.

"Come in."

Archie was working in shirtsleeves on some papers at his desk. It had been over a week since she had last seen him, and she noticed a healthy new growth of beard covering the lower half of his face. She wasn't sure how she felt about that. When he looked up and saw her, his narrow face creased in a smile, his teeth bright against the dark of his beard. "Murphy," for some reason he had settled on calling her by her last name. "Ain't you a sight for sore eyes … 'which heaven to gaudy day denies.'"

She stared at him blankly. The juxtaposition of a homely greeting with what sounded high-class English pronounced with a hill country accent momentarily non-plussed her.

"Huh? What the hell kind of greeting is that?"

"He grinned. "Thank Byron. Have a seat. What can I do for you this fine morning?"

Byron? Where did that come from? She settled onto one of the straight-backed gray metal chairs in front of his cluttered desk. "Forget Byron. You ever hear of a Lawrence Terrell?"

The name was instantly familiar to Archie. Two vertical lines appeared between his eyes. "Why do you ask? That boy disappeared a long time ago."

"Well, he's back now, and he wants to hire us for a job. I want to check him out before I decide."

"Uh huh," he grunted. "Weird. Do you know anything about the Terrell family?"

"All I know is that they are hot shit here in Charlotte. I also know that

Lawrence's father, James Terrell, went missing around ten years ago."

He nodded. "Yep, he sure did, eleven years ago, in fact, but that wasn't the beginning of the Terrell problems. No reason you should have heard about it up there in Yankee land, but it did make the national news at the time."

"What did your investigation turn up about the father's disappearance?"

"Not a damn thing. There were unconfirmed sightings of James Terrell in the Caribbean and elsewhere, but nothing panned out. After a while, things quieted down, and people went on with their lives." Archie leaned back in his chair, twirling a pencil in one hand. "Everyone suspected the wife and his brother had something to do with it, but there was no evidence. Charlotte's country club set had a field day speculating about it. The wife and brother were friendly between the sheets and did away with the husband, so the story goes. The between the sheets thing is probably true seeing as how they moved in together and got married a year later."

So far, everything Archie had said matched Lawrence Terrell's story.

"How did they do that? I thought seven years had to pass before a missing person could be declared legally dead."

"You're forcing me to dredge up stuff from my pre-Law studies at UNC. You see, normally the court requires some sort of service or legal notification to the non-filing spouse in a divorce, but once the filing spouse has exhausted all efforts and received the approval of the court, the requirement can be satisfied through what is known as 'Service by Publication.' That means you just run a newspaper ad notifying the missing spouse. And that's it. That's what Mrs. Terrell did."

The legalese was delivered with a twang that would have been at home on the Grand Old Opry stage.

"So, she divorced her missing and possibly dead husband." Krystal was so absorbed by the Terrell story that she almost missed what he had said.

"Pre-Law? You studied law?"

The man was ever full of surprises. He was the kind of guy one might picture with a beat-up baseball cap permanently affixed to his head, sucking a straw and fishing for catfish on a riverbank.

"Yep."

"So, you have a law degree?"

He looked slightly embarrassed, as if he regretted sharing the information, and ran his fingers through his closely cropped, straw colored hair.

"Yep. Thanks to the GI Bill."

"You're a lawyer?"

"Well, I passed the Bar, but I'm not really a lawyer. You might have noticed that I'm a cop," he flashed a lopsided grin.

For a few seconds she was speechless as she pondered the man's depths, and then another thought struck her. "You said James Terrell's disappearance wasn't the beginning of the Terrell problems. What do you mean?"

He laid the pencil on his desk and leaned forward to rest on his elbows, suddenly somber as he retrieved the memory. "There was an incident a week before James went missing. It may or may not be related to his disappearance, though I think it is. We received a 911 call about an emergency at the Terrell house. As it happened, I was first on the scene, and it was tragic. The daughter, Fannie, had been found floating face down in the pool by young Lawrence. I think they were around 14 at the time. They were twins. We tried CPR, but it was too late. The whole family was there around the pool with the body.

"Did you interview Lawrence?"

"I tried to, but he was so distraught we could get nothing useful from him. He was only just out of grade school at the time. The kid was in shock."

She juxtaposed the first impression Lawrence Terrell had made on her with the pitiful image Archie presented. A lot had happened to him in ten years.

"Well, he's on the warpath against his mother and uncle now, almost fanatical about it. He's certain they murdered his father and did away with the body. He even claims to have seen his uncle put his father's body in the trunk of a car."

"He claims to be an eyewitness of his uncle disposing of the body?"

She nodded. "He seems pretty sketchy, though."

Archie scratched his incipient beard. "No wonder the family kept him away from us back then."

"Maybe," she said, "but I wouldn't make any bets on it. You should see him now. There was a lot of money involved, wasn't there?"

"You bet there was. Lawrence Terrell was born into one of the wealthiest families in Charlotte. I'm talking old money here. The Terrell fortune was made in the textile industry in the 19th century. The family is part of Charlotte history and culture."

Krystal nodded. She was becoming familiar with all the "old money" circulating in Charlotte and the influence it wielded. "The kid has one thing going for his theory. Where there is a lot of money, there can be a lot of shenanigans. And then, if the idea that his mother was having an affair with her brother-in-law at the time of the disappearance is true, and it looks like it is, we have another motive just as strong as money."

"Yes," said Archie. "And don't think their being together didn't raise some dust. Lawrence isn't the only one who suspects foul play. There are people who still won't speak to them. Mary Terrell's family disowned her, so the rumor goes."

"It all seems just so Southern Gothic, doesn't it?"

"Like the song says, 'that's what I like about the South.'"

"Would you mind if we looked into the case?"

"Hey, if you guys can come up with something we missed, have at it. Curry won't be too pleased, but who cares?" he grinned. She decided the new beard lent him a rakish air.

She decided she liked the beard.

She smiled back at him. "Would it be possible to see the files?"

"I don't see why not. What the Chief doesn't know won't hurt him." Archie winked. "I'll pull what we have out of Cold Cases and bring it to you. That way Curry won't get wind of your interest. Make all the copies you want. But you'll have to share whatever you dig up with me. And if the kid still insists he saw his father's body dumped into a car trunk and you think he's credible, I'll have to talk to him sooner or later."

"You're a champ, Archie."

"Southern hospitality," he grinned. "Speaking of which, after you're read in, we can discuss the case over dinner. My treat."

The idea appealed to her. She felt unaccountably happy as she drove back to the PSI offices.

*****

Sergeant Archie Wolf clasped his hands over his head in a silent sign of victory after the auburn-haired ex-cop left his office. As their relationship, friendship – whatever it was – developed and grew over the months since her arrival in Charlotte, she had begun to occupy more and more of his thoughts. He recognized the sure signs that he was falling for her.

He had his doubts, though, about chances for success. He thought he could match her intelligence, but attractive had never been a word anyone would use to describe Archie Wolf. His lanky frame did not readily convey an impression of strength, though his wiry muscles were strong and hard as iron. Although he had taken many steps to improve himself, he could not escape the country twang in his voice which combined with his physiognomy to project the image of a dyed in the wool redneck. Since he could not conceal it, he had embraced his redneck origins. He was what he was, and that should be good enough for anybody.

Despite first appearances, Archie had had success with women … if success could include two divorces. Now at 40, it had been a long time since Archie Wolf was seriously attracted to a woman. The failed marriages had created a certain reticence to permit himself to succumb to the enticement of a lasting relationship. But despite such misgivings he felt himself on a slippery slope with Krystal Murphy.

They had become friendly, and shared some meals, but these invariably were centered around professional interests. Intimacy was not even a blip on the radar. Certainly, there was mutual respect. They were comfortable with one another, but did that mean compatibility? He was reluctant to take the next step, and that was because she had shown not even a glimmer of romantic interest and because he feared losing the relationship.

CHAPTER 4

The next day, Robert Strachey invited her to take a seat while he fiddled with a slim cigar she identified from the distinctive brown band with white lettering as a Cuban Montecristo. He clipped the end with a metallic gizmo and held the flame from a battered silver Dupont lighter to the tip. She didn't interrupt what she knew was a sacred ritual for her partner.

Strachey was in his shirtsleeves, loosened tie, and sleeves rolled to his elbows revealing a vintage Rolex GMT Master on his left wrist. Now nearing 50, hair streaked with gray, Strachey had lost none of the athleticism of his youth, the result, she knew, of a strict regimen of exercise and jogging. Over six feet tall, ruggedly handsome, not to mention rich, Strachey was a remarkably down-to-earth family man. His wife, Amy, had become Krystal's best friend. And she was his junior partner at PSI.

The cigar ignited to his satisfaction, Strachey blew on the end until it glowed orange and then drew on it and exhaled. A shaft of light from the window skewered a layer of blue smoke as it drifted across the room. Strachey returned his attention to Krystal.

"What's up?" he asked.

The impression Terrell made on her was more than a little strange, and she had her doubts about a decade old disappearance which the police had relegated to cold cases. But she had accepted the temporary retainer check, and it had not bounced. She had spent the evening reviewing the cold case files Archie had given her but found nothing more than what she knew already.

"I'm still not so sure about taking the case," she said. "I think we'll end up chasing our asses."

"The worst that could happen is that we end up the same as the police. In the meantime, we have a paying client."

"But if we don't envision success, wouldn't that be unethical? PSI has a reputation to uphold."

"Look, it's up to the client. If you explain to him that it's unlikely we will come up with anything new or definitive and he still wants to retain us, we should be happy to take his money." Strachey smiled his usual dazzling smile and drew in more rich Montecristo smoke.

She was still reluctant. "If you say so, but I think it will be a waste of my time." She immediately worried that she sounded self-important, but Strachey didn't seem to notice.

"Think of the Benjamins," he said. "This is a business like any other." Strachey might be a former CIA operative who had once spent his time saving the world, but he had become a shrewd businessman. PSI profits were healthy. Most classic gumshoe operations were relatively low on the profit chart, but occasionally one like this came along.

The idea of fighting crime for profit was still new to her, but she was getting used to it. Her standard of living had improved markedly since leaving the Arlington County Police and moving to Charlotte even if her personal life had not.

PSI had grown more quickly than she had expected. Her own reputation, most recently for having solved a notorious homicide case involving members of a prominent Charlotte family, played no small part in this. But she had to admit that Robert Strachey's uncle's local connections were mostly responsible. His recommendations counted heavily with the city's nabobs, and PSI had secured several lucrative contracts to provide security services, both technical and physical, for Charlotte enterprises.

With growth came more responsibility. While Robert managed sophisticated security jobs and the occasional overseas gig, Krystal was responsible for the gumshoe work, although this was much more than tracking down straying spouses, missing persons, and stolen property. Sometimes the victims of crimes did not believe the police were giving the old college try and hoped the firm could make more progress on their cases. And there was a lot of more prosaic work which simply required muscle rather than investigation. This included providing bouncers for night spots and bars, bodyguards, and drivers hired by suspicious parents to chaperone their children on prom nights.

Cops were always happy for off-duty employment, and Krystal's friend, Archie Wolf was more than happy to send officers eager to moonlight from his department her way. She also had hired several retired cops on both full-time and part-time bases.

The permanent staff had swollen beyond the capacity of its present office space, so most of the new folk were contract employees who did not have to work out of the office. Also, there was now a sizable IT contingent which had become one of the company's top income earners, especially during the Covid scare.

Strachey leaned back in his chair, again drawing on the cigar. "Hey, Red," he drawled, "it could be another murder case. That's right down your alley. Where do you intend to start?"

"Archie Wolf bootlegged the Cold Case files for me. Mrs. Terrell reported her husband missing two days after he disappeared. She claimed he told her he had a meeting in Asheville and might not return the same night."

"Who was the meeting with?"

"The police have no idea, and neither did Mrs. Terrell. But James Terrell's car was found several days later in a parking garage in Asheville."

"Was there anything in the car?"

"Nothing but James Terrell's prints. There was no sign of foul play."

"How about GPS tracking?"

"This was a decade ago, and it was an even older car. So, nothing."

"Were any suspects turned up?"

"Yes, but nothing came of it. All the cops had their suspicions, but there was no solid evidence."

"Tell me."

"It all comes down to motive, and that's what our client bases his accusations on, as well as claiming to have seen his uncle load his father's body into the trunk of a car. That memory may or may not be spurious. He was just a kid at the time. He blames his mother and his uncle Randolph. All of Charlotte believes the two were having an affair at the time of the disappearance. Randolph was a widower and closer in age to James's wife than his brother. And they did get married."

"How about money?"

"James Terrell was wealthy, incredibly so, but so was his younger brother. When daddy died, he left the real-estate business to James and the textile business to Randolph. If Randolph had a motive to kill his brother, it wasn't money."

"That leaves love," said Strachey.

"Why not just divorce? Especially if money was not a problem."

"You think there must be something deeper here? Did James and Randolph hate one another?"

"No clue."

CHAPTER 5

I live back in the woods you see,
My woman and the kids and the dogs and me
I got a shotgun, a rifle, and a four-wheel drive,
And a country boy can survive,
Country folks can survive.

Hank Williams, Jr.

It was quiet in the chill expectation of dawn, the time when sleep is soundest.

The sturdy log home stood in a clearing in the middle of a heavily wooded property with a half-mile-long gravel drive leading from the main road through thick pine and the occasional white oak or maple. It was a large house with a red tin roof and a spacious gravel-covered parking area in front where a new Ford F-150 and a battered Jeep Wrangler stood. There were steps leading to a small, covered porch and the screened front door. Large stones had been laid to create a meandering border along the front of the porch where shrubs and rose bushes were planted.

The waning moon cast soft shadows across the parking area, and the stillness was disturbed only by the hoot of an owl, startled by two men moving carefully through the woods toward the log home.

The tranquil scene had a greenish hue through the night vision optics worn by the two men. They moved with practiced ease, keeping to the natural cover until it ended at the edge of the parking area about twenty feet from the house.

The sun would not rise for another hour, by which time they would have returned to the car where their leader waited on the road below the house. They remained in place for several minutes observing the house for signs of movement or alarm.

The two men were experienced in this type of operation from action they had seen in the Middle East and Ukraine. Assaults such as the one now before them were usually successful before dawn when the targets would be sleeping the most soundly. And best of all, the people in this house had no idea they were targets.

There was a dog on the premises, a coffee-colored Labrador, which would bark a warning as the men rushed the house. But surprise and speed were on their side, and the occupants of the house, and the dog too, would be dealt with while they were still groggy from sleep.

There were four human targets: a man, his wife, and two children. The nature of the targets did not concern them. They had a job to do, one they had done before, and mercy was not a consideration.

They had chosen AR-15s for this job. The semi-automatic rifles could spit out an amazing number of .223 rounds in a short amount of time. They were proficient in the use of more specialized, even exotic fully automatic weapons, but the commonality of the .223 ammunition so widely used in this part of the world for hunting and recreation would provide the authorities with a plethora of suspects.

There were two security cameras mounted on the front of the house and the men wore balaclavas to mask their features. The cameras were wireless and thus not easily disabled and might be remotely monitored. For this reason, they were not wearing their customary military clothing but were dressed simply in jeans and heavy, dark shirts – normal attire for this rural Georgia county. Even if the security system alerted local authorities, the house was remote and isolated. They would set the house ablaze before they left. A lot of time would pass before local law enforcement could get there, affording them plenty of time to clear the area. Easy-peasy.

A pre-operational rush of adrenalin charged their systems with anticipatory excitement. They nodded at one another and sprinted across the parking area, covering the short distance in a few seconds. A deep bark issued from somewhere inside the house as lights triggered by motion sensors flooded the area, prompting the men to quickly remove their night vision gear on the run. One of them, his AR slung over one shoulder, carried a steel battering ram which he employed immediately, smashing it into the doorknob and lock of the front door with shattering force, and the door flew open.

With his companion close behind, the first man stepped into the dark interior. Almost immediately, there were two loud reports, and he stumbled backward out the door into his surprised partner who was knocked back down the steps where he landed on his back.

Simultaneously, a tall, bearded man in pajamas raced from around the side of the house. He carried a Mossberg 940 Pro Tactical shotgun at the ready. The Mossberg is semi-automatic and carries 7+1 rounds. Without pausing he fired two 12-gauge loads of double ought buckshot into the second intruder before he could regain his feet, and then fired two more at the first who had grabbed a porch post for support. He was propelled onto his face by the blast and lay sprawled, unmoving.

The bearded man cautiously approached the man on the ground who now lay groaning, spilling copious amounts of blood over the gravel of the parking area. The first rounds had caught him in the side, serious, possibly fatal wounds, but he was still moving. Still clutching his AR-15, he rolled toward the bearded man who raised the Mossberg again and fired point blank erasing the intruder's face and part of his skull.

He walked to the body and prodded it with his toe. Satisfied, he looked up at the house where a slim, blond woman in a flannel nightgown stood holding a Glock 21 .45 caliber pistol in a professional two-handed grip pointed at the body on the porch. She kicked the body, satisfied herself the man was dead, and said, "You didn't need to shoot him, Frank, I plugged him good the first time."

The bearded man said, "It's over, honey. These sumbitches ain't gonna bother us again."

CHAPTER 6

Yuriy Volodin waited in a rented SUV at the bottom of the drive. The operation should take no more than a few minutes once his men entered the house. The residence was isolated, so it would be some time before the bodies were discovered. By then, he and his team would be far away. He smiled as he foresaw the chagrin of the local constabulary as they tried to unravel what had happened.

Dawsonville, Georgia, population 3,500, was hardly a thriving metropolitan area with a large police force. Dawson County was covered by the County Sheriff's office, and Volodin doubted their abilities. The Sheriff would call in outside help, the State Police, or the Georgia Bureau of Investigations. Volodin's men were careful. They would leave no clues other than misleading ones, a torched house, and dead bodies.

Volodin did not consider the elimination of an entire family murder or a moral outrage. No, it was an assignment, pure and simple. Justified retribution from an angry Russian leader for the destruction of an important operation. Who the targets were was immaterial.

The distant sound of gunfire reached him through the trees. The reports did not sound like the AR-15's his men carried. He recognized the report of a shotgun fired repeatedly and was immediately concerned when there were no answering reports from the AR-15's. When silence settled over the pre-dawn gray with no more noise coming from the house, Volodin was in a quandary. Should he go up the hill and see what had happened? No. Whoever fired the shotgun might well be coming downhill toward him right now.

He waited a few more seconds, hoping to see his men emerge from the woods, but when they did not appear, Volodin sped away. He was an unhappy camper. He had not liked this assignment from the beginning, considering it pointless. The Americans had compromised an important Russian influence operation. So what? This was hardly the first time Russia had suffered an intelligence failure.

He thought back to his meeting with Colonel General Klichkov.

*****

Yuriy Volodin's appearance was striking – tall and thin with a shaved skull. But it was his eyes that everyone who met him remembered. They were deep set and intensely blue, like twin sapphires glowing inside a cave, and when he fixed his gaze upon you, the effect was much like being an insect pinned to a board. The uncomfortable object of his attention now was his boss, Colonel General Aleksey Klichkov of the FSB, Russia's Federal Security Service.

The two of them sat in Klichkov's large office at the headquarters of the FSB's Center for Special Operations, also known as Unit 35690, in Balashikha, a town about fifteen miles east of Moscow. In Soviet times, the center served as the military base for the KGB's Vympel Spetsnaz unit. That unit was now under the control of the FSB and redesignated Department V. Its sister Spetsnaz unit, the "Alfa" group, now the FSB's Department A, shared the facility.

Nearly eighteen months earlier, Yuriy had been recalled from an undercover assignment in the United States which had ended in disaster and forced Yuriy to kill the FSB's number one American asset. The operation had been as costly as it had been ambitious, involving the suborning of several members of the American Congress and the media with the goal of enabling Moscow to interfere in the American electoral process and promote policies damaging to the United States, still Russia's "main enemy."

The assignment had not been to Yuriy's liking. His cover forced him to live in seedy Brighton Beach in Brooklyn among an émigré population he disdained. And he liked even less the person he had been sent to support -- a former high-ranking CIA officer named Paul Wakefield who treated him like a subordinate.

Yuriy was not new to "wet work." He had earned great respect from his service in Afghanistan as a very young Spetsnaz, or special ops, soldier, and more recently in Chechnya, Syria, and Ukraine. Ironically, his last kill in the United States had been Paul Wakefield who had been captured by the FBI and would surely have spilled his guts to them to save himself. The FSB could not allow that to happen. As usual, Yuriy carried out his assignment successfully and escaped.

Now Klichkov wanted to send him back.

"You must understand, Yuriy, that it is not our decision. I agree with you that retaliation at such a low level is meaningless and gains us nothing. But the president feels differently. He's getting his ass kicked in Ukraine, and he wants something to feel good about. The Wakefield operation was important to him, and he takes the failure as a personal insult. So, you see we have no choice, and quite simply put, you are the best man for the job. You are already familiar with the targets."

"This is an unnecessary risk," growled Yuriy. "And it's been over a year now. Why now?"

Klichkov shook his head. "I know, Yuriy, believe me, I know. But the president hates the Americans, and the disaster we suffered in Washington was a significant set-back for him. And now Ukraine is falling apart. It's personal for him. He needs a victory. He wants to hurt the Americans, send them a message. The idea of delayed but devastating retribution appeals to him. The Americans will be taken totally by surprise."

"Why us? Why not the GRU?" Volodin thought he already knew the answer.

Klichkov smiled. “The president has lost faith in the GRU’s Unit 29155. They’ve screwed up every operation they’ve undertaken and embarrassed themselves and Russia. The Skripal affair was a disaster. No, the president wants us. He is a former director of the FSB, after all. And, Volodin, you performed well in America despite everything else.”

“It was all Wakefield’s fault,” Yuriy grumbled. “And it wasn’t even American counterintelligence which uncovered his activities. It was a simple cop, and a woman at that. Wakefield was self-important and overconfident. He made bad choices. It’s a failed operation. We should forget it and move on.”

Klichkov spread his arms. “Nevertheless, Yuriy …”

“’Ours is not to reason why …?’” Yuriy expelled a long sigh of exasperation. The president was taking things personally, something a wise leader should know better than to do. He was fast losing faith and trust in the president, who seemed increasingly unstable, and the people around him were beginning to take note. Finally, he asked, “How do I get back into the United States?”

The general was relieved. Conversations with Yuriy Volodin were always difficult. The man's very presence made even other Department V operatives nervous. "We're arranging that with our friends in Venezuela and the Sinaloa Cartel," he replied. "They will get you and your team across the border as well as any equipment you need. They will arrange for transportation, as well. You should pick two men you trust, men who speak some English. The way you carry out your orders is, of course, entirely up to you. But we hope you can accomplish the task quickly, and we will extract you back across the border into Mexico. While in the United States, you will be supported by one of our illegals. He was placed in North Carolina several months ago with the task of locating your targets. Your success will earn the eternal gratitude of the president." He smiled broadly and stood to indicate the meeting was at an end.

Yuriy stood as well. Ignoring Klichkov's outstretched hand, he said, "I'll take a couple of the men I worked with in Ukraine. I'll send you their names so you can bring them back here."

Klichkov watched as the tall assassin limped out of his office. Volodin had suffered a serious leg wound from a Mujahedeen bullet many years ago in Afghanistan. It brought to mind Klichkov's favorite Sherlock Holmes stories and Watson's jezail bullet, but Volodin was no affable Dr. Watson.

CHAPTER 7

If there was one person in Charlotte who was a reliable source of high society gossip, it was Strachey's aunt Sadie. She was married to his uncle Lyle, who had become a successful attorney in Charlotte and an even more successful lobbyist for Southern business interests in Washington. Despite Lyle having to spend a lot of time in Washington, the couple maintained their family home in the venerable Myers Park neighborhood.

Charlotte is a bustling metropolis, the most populous city in the state. It boasts professional sports teams, NASCAR, and a major golf tournament. Lots of northerners are attracted there by the commerce and banking giants such as Wells Fargo and Bank of America. But the newcomers have not yet penetrated old Charlotte society which is populated by folks who still employ the honeyed North Carolina accent.

The old ways were already retreating before the invasion of the non-Southern with their loose manners and even looser morals. Even so, beneath its superficial glitter there remains a core of the old families, the real Charlotteans, and Sadie Strachey was one of the stalwarts. Although her husband was a relative newcomer to the city, Sadie's family could trace its origins there all the way back to the 18th century beginnings of the "Queen City." Her husband's family came from the Southern Appalachian mill town of Canton, but when she first set eyes on ambitious, up-and-coming attorney Lyle Strachey, she knew he was the one for her. Her sharp eye and intuition paid off as Lyle built a fortune and the huge home in Myers Park for her.

After her morning confabulation with Strachey, Krystal drove from the city center to tree-bedecked Myers Park. Modernity was invading even here where many of the old, large brick colonial homes were being demolished and replaced by 6,000 square foot Italianate villas. Krystal preferred the staid, older homes, but ideas of how to display wealth were changing. Ostentation was replacing taste.

She parked in the cement drive in front of the huge, white stone house. She had called ahead, so Aunt Sadie was waiting at the door and stepped outside to greet her. Sadie had grown fond of the athletic, green-eyed redhead and gave her a hug and a peck on the cheek. Her costume of choice for the day was white Capri pants and a bright red blouse, with red strap-on sandals. For a lady somewhere in her late sixties her face was remarkably unlined, which Krystal unkindly ascribed to Botox, and her exquisitely highlighted blond hair cut in a polished bob betrayed no sign of gray. In her youth, the diminutive Sadie would have been in the vernacular of the times "something else." The calendar girl good looks, however, concealed a first-rate mind.

"Come on in, Krystal," she drawled over her shoulder heading back inside. "I've had a light lunch prepared for us out back." At the rear of the house was a paved area surrounding a kidney-shaped swimming pool, now drained, and they were soon seated at table shaded by a large umbrella from a surprisingly warm late May sun. A nearby magnolia tree was covered with pink and white blossoms. Lunch was cold chicken with a variety of raw vegetables, and sweet tea, the quintessential Southern beverage of choice.

As they began filling their plates, Sadie gave her a comically wicked grin, "Bobby called right after you did. He says you want to pump me for salacious gossip." Krystal did not believe anyone else called Robert Strachey "Bobby."

Krystal had to laugh. "That's right, as salacious as it can get. And I suspect you won't have to reach far when it comes to the Terrell family."

"Oh, my Lord," Sadie paused with a forkful of chicken suspended halfway between plate and mouth. "The Terrells. My, my, what a tragedy. I swear I'll never understand it."

"That's a promising beginning," said Krystal, sensing that Sadie was warming up to a story. "Tell me everything."

"Well," whispered Sadie, "you know that James Terrell disappeared?"

Krystal nodded as she sipped her sweet tea.

"You can just imagine how much talk there was after James disappeared. Everybody had an opinion, and there are quite a few people here in town who have known the Terrell family for a long time.

James and Mary are way younger than me. Gossip has it that James was a popular fraternity boy at Davidson College. His brother, Randolph, was a few years younger and came to campus after James. Mary came the next year if I recall. That must have been in the mid-70's. Davidson didn't have coeds until 1970. They say Randolph was immediately smitten by her. Soon enough the two brothers and Mary became an inseparable trio, and a competition of sorts sprang up between the boys for Mary's affections. In the end, Mary chose James. I think she must have thought he was more mature and worldly than Randolph."

Things were falling into place in Krystal's mind. "How did Randolph take losing out to his big brother?"

"Oh, they say he took it well. The three were, after all, good friends. I never heard of any particular rancor. But, of course, he must have been disappointed, and that sometimes turns into resentment. There was a lot of talk after James disappeared, of course."

"You are very wise," said Krystal. "That covers the early years, what about ten years ago when things hit the fan, when the daughter drowned?"

Sadie chewed on a carrot as she gathered her thoughts. "It was terrible, of course, the drowning, I mean. Such a young girl with everything to look forward to. Terrible accident. The family took it hard, especially the twin brother. And then, barely a week later, James just ups and vanishes from the face of the earth. Now, you can believe that caused some ripples on the pond. The rumor spread that Mary and Randolph were having an affair, and that led to all sorts of dark suspicions. Did James run away out of grief for his drowned daughter? Or was it because his wife and brother were seeing one another behind his back? Or," she paused for dramatic effect before leaning over the table to say in an exaggerated stage whisper, "did Mary and Randolph murder James and do away with his body? There are still lots of people who think that is what happened, especially because Randolph up and married Mary before the body was cold, to coin a phrase."

"Is there anything besides rumors?" asked Krystal.

Sadie tilted her head in thought for a few beats. "Well, you know that the textile industry dried up here in North Carolina.

Randolph ended up outsourcing everything to someplace in Asia where they still have slave labor. On the other hand, real estate remains profitable, especially if you own a lot of choice buildings in town along Tryon Street. With James gone, Randolph got control of the real estate side of the family business."

Sadie picked up another carrot stick and chewed thoughtfully for a minute. "You should speak with Agatha May Caldwell. She's the same age as Mary, and they have been friends since college. If there is anyone who has any dirt on Mary, it's Agatha May, for sure. I'll give her a jingle and let her know you're coming, if you like. That should clear the way for you."

"Do it, please," said Krystal.

On the way back to the office, she considered Sadie's information. It had all the characteristics of a TV soap opera which had run for years with still no end in sight. Maybe Agatha May Caldwell could provide a coherent plot line. Sadie had provided the address and promised to call.

Krystal would call on Caldwell later in the afternoon. Discretion was called for. She was dealing with a sensitive and explosive issue, and there was good reason at this stage to avoid publicity regarding the investigation, if only to protect Randolph and Mary Terrell should they prove innocent of any wrongdoing, and they might well be. This was not the first time Krystal had seen a case where the most likely suspects turned out to be innocent. She now had sufficient background to proceed, thanks to Archie Wolf and Aunt Sadie.

CHAPTER 8

It was nearly two o'clock when Krystal returned to the office after her interview with Aunt Sadie. Ruth Scatterfield met her entrance with a wide grin. "Bob wants to see you in his office," she beamed. "He said you should go right in."

"What's up?" asked Krystal, suspicious of the receptionist's poorly concealed glee. There wasn't much to smile about these days.

"You'll see. Just go on now." Ruth giggled like a nine-year-old girl.

At least it didn't appear to be more unwelcome news. She gave a perfunctory rap on Strachey's door and went in. Strachey was standing by the window talking to a tall, gangly man with a mane of graying hair that hung to his shoulders. Both were puffing on cigars. The visitor was dressed in biker gear, jeans, boots, and a leather vest with the Harley Davidson logo emblazoned on its back. Even with his back to her, the figure was immediately recognizable.

"Frank Watson!" she exclaimed.

Watson turned, grinned broadly, and strode quickly to her. He embraced her in a bear hug that lifted her off her feet. Lowering her gently to the floor, he planted a hairy kiss on her cheek. "Hello, Red," he said, "You are surely a sight for sore eyes."

Strachey's eyes widened. He had never seen anyone take such liberties with his fiery partner.

Recovering her breath, Krystal took a step back and surveyed the six-foot four visitor. Besides the long hair, Watson sported a thick beard, and even now in May the part of his face not covered in whiskers was more tanned and weather-beaten than she remembered, probably due to high speeds on a motorcycle.

Frank Watson was an old friend and ex-cop from Arlington who had partnered with her and Strachey on a particularly dangerous case involving the CIA, FBI, politicians, and Russian spies. He was one of only two people who called her "Red." The other was Robert Strachey. His long hair and general appearance announced none too subtly that Frank was no longer employed by the Arlington County Police Department.

"So, you did finally retire," she said.

"Yup. Couldn't take it anymore. The fun left the job when you abandoned us to the guvvies and politicians."

"You took the family back to Georgia, I suppose."

"Sho' nuff. Bought a little spread just outside of Dawsonville. Been happy as a pig in shit."

Krystal had become accustomed to Frank Watson's fondness for pithy aphorisms and countrified wisdom. To judge from his greeting, his return to Georgia had reinforced the habit. Watson, she knew, was an intelligent man and great cop. He just relished affecting a backwoods persona.

"Did you get that small town sheriff's job you were talking about?"

"Sort of. The sheriff's job is an elected position, and it'll take the locals a little while to learn how lovable I am. But the county sheriff's office did have an opening. I'm one of their investigators - part time."

"Good for you. Not that I'm not glad to see you, but what brings you up here to the big city?"

A shadow passed over Watson's creased face erasing the bonhomie. "Something not so nice, Red. Something that concerns you, and ole Bob here, as well."

Strachey interjected, "Why don't we all sit down while Frank explains." He motioned them to the couch and leather upholstered chairs in the corner of his office. "Can I offer you a drink, Frank?"

"You got bourbon?"

"I'm a scotch guy, but I always have bourbon for friends. Blanton's OK with you?"

Watson's eyebrows shot up. "You might be a scotch guy, but you got good taste in bourbon."

"Blanton's it is, then." Strachey crossed to the wet bar and pulled glasses and bottles from the shelf. For himself, he selected Ardbeg Uigeadail with a touch of water.

Watson turned an inquisitive eye to Krystal. “You ain’t havin’ nuthin?”

“Not now, Frank, thanks.” She asked Strachey for a coke.

Watson eyed quizzically her for a moment and asked, “You OK, Red?”

Her old partner knew her too well. “Yeah, no problems. I just feel like a coke. It’s still a little early in the day for me.” She didn’t want to explain herself to Frank just now. Maybe later. She had always valued his advice.

A year earlier when her drinking worried her friends, Strachey had offered to put an end to the daily happy hour in his office. He had a well-stocked wet bar and had instituted the habit of inviting co-workers to an after-hours libation. Krystal had refused to allow him to curtail a practice he and others enjoyed so much. She could take care of her own problem.

Once they had settled into their seats, Watson began. “A couple of weeks ago I got the feelin’ that someone was following me. He was good, but I got that itchy feelin’ on the back of my neck, and I got sort of sneaky. It took a couple of days to confirm there was at least two of ‘em, big guys with short haircuts. They followed me up to the house one day and then just drove on past the driveway.

"Well, it seemed to me like those two fellers was up to no good, and that sat in my craw like hair in a biscuit. So, I set some silent alarms around the house out in the woods so there would be plenty of warning if anybody come sneakin' up there. Sho 'nuff, just a coupla days later, here they come, real early in the mornin'. We put the kids in the basement, my wife grabbed her .45 and waited in the house while I snuck out the back way with my Mossberg. Them ole boys got a big surprise when they tried to break in. It was the last surprise either of 'em ever got. They got the red licked off their candy right down to the hard center."

"Jeez, Frank" breathed Krystal, "that's crazy."

Watson drained his bourbon. "Can I have another?" He held his glass out to Strachey, who splashed more bourbon into it. Watson took another sip and continued. "Them egg suckers wasn't from anywhere around Dawsonville. They wasn't even from Georgia. The FBI ran some GBIA tests on 'em, and guess what?" He shook his head. "They was Russians."

Krystal and Strachey looked at one another as each had the same thought.

Watson chuckled, “I figgered that’d get your attention. Now for the good part.” He turned to Krystal. “A couple of days ago I got a call from your old FBI buddy Enoch Whitehall. He’s worried about us.” Watson shot a look at Krystal before continuing. “He thinks, judging from the attack on me, the Russkies is out for revenge for Wakefield’s death. There just ain’t no other reason some Russkies would be tryin’ to kill someone like me. The Wakefield thing is the closest I ever got to a Russian. Whitehall told me to skedaddle up here right quick and warn you to start bein’ real careful. There is likely more of them guys.”

Strachey absorbed this information with a solemn mien. “Well, I’ll be damned. I never thought we would hear Wakefield’s name again. It’s a stretch, but Whitehall might have the right idea. And if he does, there are likely more bad guys out there than the two you eliminated.”

Watson scratched his head. “Well, them two had to get to my place somehow, and I didn’t find anyone else when I looked. I figger someone had to drive them there, and he took off when the shootin' was over."

Strachey nodded. "That's a reasonable assumption." He turned to Krystal. "They'll be after you, too, Krystal."

The memories washed over her leaving a cold chill in their wake. George Wakefield was a former senior CIA officer with extensive experience in Latin America who had gone rogue. In collaboration with Russian intelligence, he had contrived to subvert members of Congress and the media to do their bidding. Krystal, Strachey, and Watson had become entangled in the affair through what had started as a routine murder investigation. Krystal and Watson would have been killed by Wakefield's mercenaries had they not been rescued at the last moment by Strachey and the FBI's Hostage Rescue Team at a remote site in St. Michaels, Maryland.

Feeling a bit overwhelmed, she said, "Jeez, Frank. I'm sorry." Krystal wasn't sure why she should be sorry, but it's what she said. "I would never have imagined."

"Tell you what, Red. Nuthin' to be sorry about." Watson grinned. "Fact of the matter, shootin' them guys just cranked some more lead in my pencil."

This vintage Watsonism elicited a grin from Krystal. Frank Watson had been her first supervisor and mentor on the Arlington County Police force, and years of collaboration and friendship had taught her that there was a sharp intelligence behind the country boy façade. His speech had reverted to pure country following his retirement.

She turned to Strachey. "So, there is a team of Russian killers after all of us?"

"It seems possible," he nodded. "An attempted massacre of Frank and his family by two Russian nationals can't be ignored. And Whitehall might know more than he's saying."

"I thought the entire Wakefield episode had been tamped down," said Krystal. "Whitehall made us all sign that non-disclosure agreement."

"Sure," said Strachey, "but we're all professionals. I guess it was inevitable that there would be leaks once the congressional committees were briefed, our identities revealed. Those assholes could never keep a secret, and who knows if the Russians still have sources on Capitol Hill? And the FBI itself has become a prolific source of politically motivated leaks."

"I'll bet Whitehall is fit to be tied," said Watson. "He's a scary guy. And how old is he, anyway? There was a picture of him and J. Edgar Hoover on his office wall! They was both holdin' Tommy guns."

"I have no idea how old he is," said Krystal, "and I doubt anyone else does either." Enoch Whitehall, the FBI's Executive Assistant Director for Counterintelligence, was a legend, and no one could say how long he had held that position.

"So, what's the plan?" asked Watson.

CHAPTER 9

Strachey decided to send his family to stay with his father in Canton, the Appalachian town where he had grown up in western North Carolina, until the situation was resolved. His role in the Wakefield affair had not been as direct as Krystal's and Watson's, but there had been an attempt on his life at the time back in Washington, nonetheless.

Watson insisted on accompanying Krystal home, following on his big Harley. Upon arrival at her townhouse, he announced, "I'll spend the night out here on watch. You go on in and get some sleep."

"Don't be an idiot, Sir Galahad. Grab your bag and come on in. You can watch just as well from inside where it's a helluva lot safer, and you can catch 40 winks on my couch."

Watson didn't argue and followed her inside where he insisted on checking every room.

"I'll fix something for us to eat. The bathroom is up those stairs, first door on your left, if you want to freshen up."

"Pretty fancy digs you got here, Red." Watson approvingly surveyed the living room."

"The pay is a little better here than it was in Arlington," she shouted from the kitchen. I bought all new stuff when I moved in here. Bob gave me a big advance."

"You kept all your cow gewgaws I see." Watson admired the collection of bovine figurines and photos of Krystal's childhood on the family farm in Indiana.

"Keeps me grounded." She heated some leftover Kentucky Fried Chicken in the microwave and made a salad. She placed everything on the dining table. "Want some sweet tea?"

"You're going hard-core Southern, ain't you. Sweet tea! I wouldn't have believed it."

"When in Rome," she said.

*****

Krystal spent a restless night recalling the grisly details of the Wakefield case. The events that led to Wakefield's death and the quiet resignations of several members of Congress had begun with the murder of a young lawyer and ended with a dramatic shoot-out at Wakefield's private compound on the shores of the Chesapeake Bay in St. Michaels, Maryland. All that had unfolded over two years ago, and it was a shock to discover that it still reverberated.

But tomorrow was another day, and regardless of Watson's unwelcome news, she would continue investigating the Terrell case. There was a lot to do, and she was too deep into the case to drop it now. Despite Watson's conjectures, she wondered if there really were more Russian assassins out there. If there were, maybe they had been scared off by what had happened at Watson's place. She had asked Watson if it was wise to leave his family alone, but he assured her that the local sheriff had placed a guard at his property. Besides, he had grinned, his wife was perfectly capable of taking care of herself and the kids.

He had winked and grinned and in a surprisingly pleasing baritone intoned a lyric from his favorite song: "A country boy can survive."

Well, Krystal Murphy could take care of herself, too. This wasn't her first rodeo with killers.

After confirming that Aunt Sadie had called ahead, she drove to the Caldwell address. Despite her complaints, Watson insisted on accompanying her. She was faintly amused by the hirsute Georgian's concern, but wondered how long he would remain at her side. Eventually, he would have to go back to his family.

Agatha May Caldwell lived in an expansive, modern home on Colville Road in Eastover, a suburb southeast of the city center which was touted to be Charlotte's premier neighborhood. Krystal had long ago discovered that everyone in town considered their neighborhood to be supreme. She'd given up comparing them because it simply did not matter to her. Growing up on a farm in rural Indiana had given her the Hoosier's typically phlegmatic perspective on questions of class and wealth.

Watson insisted on going with her and remained in the car. She walked to the front door, enjoying the warmth of the Spring sun on her face. Spring got warm in the South much faster than it did in the Washington area, another invidious comparison that she found quite easy to make. She really was planting some roots in Charlotte.

She rang the bell, and the door was opened a moment later by a woman in her mid to late 40's, bottle blonde, and carefully applied make-up that would put Dolly Parton to shame. She was slightly plump and should not have been wearing skinny jeans, but she was, accompanied by a red silk blouse with one too many buttons undone. There were several gold bangles around her wrists and a bejeweled cross hung from a gold chain around her neck. She had the harried aspect of a quiz show contestant who couldn't come up with the right answer with time running out. She gave Krystal a rapid once-over and barraged her with questions about menus.

CHAPTER 10

It was a busy day for Agatha May Caldwell. Her daughter, Tandy May, was engaged to be married to a highly eligible young man, and the date was scarcely over a month away. There was so much to do, and even a month did not seem like enough time. Ellie Cochran, the wedding planner, was in the house today, and a sales representative was showing three gowns from the Justin Alexander Collection to Tandy Lee and her maid of honor. She expected the menu planner to ring the bell at any moment. She vowed to be firm with him. Guests at her daughter's wedding would not be served overcooked salmon and rubber chicken. She was satisfied that the rehearsal dinner she had scheduled for the swankiest restaurant in Charlotte would not disappoint. But catering at the Charlotte Country Club could be spotty. Well, she could count on the wedding planner to back her up.

This was on her mind when the doorbell rang. She checked her watch and frowned. The menu planner was early. She took that as a good sign. She did not recognize the person waiting outside the door. Had the country club sent someone new? The visitor was a tall, auburn-haired woman in a somber pantsuit, white silk blouse, sensible shoes, wearing a serious expression. Her age could have been anywhere from 25 to 35, and she was very attractive.

"Come on in," said Agatha May. "You're early."

The visitor's face betrayed mild surprise. "Early?"

"Well, of course I was expecting you an hour later." She noticed the woman was not carrying a briefcase or anything else that could contain menu suggestions. What, she wondered, was the club up to? "Where are the menu suggestions? I told the club specifically to have several alternatives for me to consider."

Finally finding an opening, Krystal said, "I think you must be mistaken. Didn't Sadie Strachey call?"

The woman, whom Krystal assumed was Agatha May Caldwell, gave her a look of consternation before recovering. "Oh, my Lord. I forgot Sadie had called. You must be the one working with her nephew. There is so much going on today. I guess I can give you some time, but not too much."

Given the multitude of concerns bedeviling her today, Agatha May would have been forgiven for begging off an interview, but the fact of the matter was she was intrigued by what Sadie had told her about the detective's interest in the Terrells. And she was a greedy devourer of cozy mysteries, often imagining she was Angela Lansbury. This was her chance to meet a real detective, and a woman at that. Were it not for the bedlam of white satin and silk, a selection of bouquets, and the impending visit of the caterer, Sadie would have happily spent the entire morning with the detective.

Krystal followed the thankfully elastic skinny jeans through the house which was alive with squeals from two young women examining what looked like wedding dresses while a wispy young man in a tight-fitting suit fluttered around them. An older woman in a tailored suit stood to one side with her arms crossed. Bouquets of different hues and compositions lay strewn about on furniture. The place reeked of barely contained hysteria.

Casting an anxious glance over her shoulder, Agatha May led her to an enclosed patio at the rear of the house and invited her to sit in one of two cushioned wicker chairs while she took the other. "I'm sorry for the way the place looks today," she said. "My daughter's wedding is next month, and we still haven't finalized the plans." She glanced at her watch. "I don't have much time. I'm expecting the caterer at any minute. Can I get you some sweet tea or a coke?"

"No, thanks," said Krystal. "I can come back at a more convenient time, if you like."

"Oh, no," breathed Agatha May. "I'll just make the time for you today. From now until the wedding, everything will be turned upside down."

She paused for breath before leaning toward Krystal and saying in a half-whisper, "Sadie said you wanted to talk about the Terrells. Has something happened? Did they find the body?"

"Er, no," replied Krystal, "we're just reviewing the matter of James Terrell's disappearance to see if the police might have missed something."

"I see," said Agatha May. "Why are you doing that?"

"We have a client who is interested in the case."

Agatha May was surprised. “Who could that be?” Her voice was eager. “Is it someone local? Do I know them? I just can’t imagine ...”

The conversation was quickly careening out of control. Krystal interrupted. “I’m sorry, but I can’t divulge the identity of our client. I was hoping you could just share with me what you know about what happened. I understand that you and Mary Terrell have been friends for some time.”

“Oh, my, yes, we have. I don’t see much of her anymore, though. Not since James disappeared.” She gave Krystal a knowing look. “She and Randolph were quietly asked to drop their membership in the Charlotte Country Club, and that’s where we used to socialize the most. It was shameful to have kicked them out. I was surprised they were admitted to the Myers Park club.”

The Charlotte Country Club was the city’s most prestigious. Krystal got the impression that Agatha May did not really think it had been so shameful. There were plenty of other places to socialize besides a country club. She pegged Agatha May as one of those people who worry more than necessary about what other people think.

"What do you think happened, Mrs. Caldwell? You were close to Mary, and you must have talked with her after the disappearance."

Agatha May said, "Well, it was strange. Mary and I met in college at Davidson. To tell the truth, neither one of us was as interested in a degree as we were in finding a man to marry. She started hanging around with Randolph and James, and I was hoping we could each snag one of the brothers. Their family was very well-to-do. But she had them both wrapped around her little finger." Agatha May frowned at the memory.

"Oh, I did go out with James once, only once. He had his hand under my blouse as soon as I got in his car. I was looking for a husband, but I wasn't going to get a reputation on campus as 'easy.' He was a handsome young man, but he was a real horndog. I warned Mary about him, but it only piqued her interest. She evidently accepted that sort of thing and either could not or would not resist him. And once she was with James, Randolph had no chance with her."

"What about Randolph?" asked Krystal. He was one of the prime suspects in his brother's disappearance and sibling rivalry over a love interest was an old story.

"Oh, Randolph," said Agatha May. She smiled at the memory. "He was not like his brother. He was a real gentleman and kind of shy. It was obvious that he was over the moon about Mary, but he kept his distance once his older brother staked his claim. The three of them remained friends, all the same."

"So," asked Krystal, "Mary never stepped out on James with Randolph?"

Agatha May's eyes lit up as she gave Krystal a sly look. She lowered her voice. "Well, not back then, but things changed, some say, even before James disappeared. Randolph's wife passed away, you know, and he never re-married ... until James was out of the way." She gave Krystal another look pregnant with innuendo and shook her head, warming to the subject. "Just imagine someone carrying a torch all those years."

"You and Mary were still close after college, weren't you? Did she ever say or do anything to make you think she was having an affair with Randolph? Did she ever say anything about her marriage?"

Agatha May was warming to the subject and that sly look crept back into her eyes. "Well, there was nothing explicit, but I could tell she was unhappy."

"When did this begin?"

"Oh, I think it was about a year before James disappeared. She just wasn't herself. I thought James must be messing around outside their marriage. He was only too aware of how attractive he was, and he was awfully flirty with other women. I asked, but Mary just clammed up. Wouldn't say a thing. Now that I think about it, she changed a lot in that last year. She seemed to just shrink into herself."

"You didn't speak with her after her husband disappeared?"

"Oh, yes. We were all sympathetic what with her daughter committing suicide and then James just up and vanishing."

"Are you sure the daughter committed suicide?" Archie Wolf had not mentioned suicide when discussing Fannie's drowning.

Agatha May's eyebrows shot upward in surprise. "Do you mean she didn't?"

Krystal immediately regretted the question. From the greedy look on Agatha May's face, it was evident she was devouring the idea of foul play associated with Fannie Terrell's death. How long would it be, she wondered, before this salacious tidbit was injected into the bloodstream of the country club gossip circuit? She tried to cover her mistake. "The police consider the drowning an accident."

Agatha May was disappointed. "Oh," she said. "Well, I should hope so."

The chimes of the doorbell sounded from the front of the house.

"That must be the caterer from the club. I just must handle this now."

Krystal stood. "I understand, so I'll be going now. Thank you so much for your time."

Agatha May accompanied her to the door. "Please don't hesitate to contact me again if I can be of more help." She opened the door to a hopeful looking young woman carrying a large folder.

Back in the car, Krystal mentally reviewed Agatha May's information. Had she learned anything new and relevant to the case? James Terrell was a "horndog," an expression she had learned in Charlotte. Had his womanizing continued after his marriage? He and Mary had been married for fifteen years before his disappearance. Maybe Mary was one of those women who treasured the institution of marriage over the fidelity of her spouse. She had been noticeably unhappy beginning a year before James disappeared. Something had happened, but what? This was yet another thread which trailed off into obscurity. And there was the question of the daughter's death. Had the child committed suicide?

CHAPTER 11

When Archie Wolf arrived that evening to pick her up for dinner, she introduced him to Frank Watson, explaining that he was an old friend and fellow cop from Arlington visiting from Georgia. She was unhappy about not telling him the truth, but Strachey had insisted that they keep things under wraps until he produced a plan of action. Strictly speaking, he had said, this was not a police matter. She didn't see it entirely that way, but reluctantly agreed with the proviso that they get their act together quickly.

She had persuaded Watson that she would be perfectly safe with Archie, and as the two men sized one another up she sensed an affinity between them. Maybe it was a redneck thing. Something she had determined about so-called rednecks: they were more perceptive on a human level than most, which enabled them to size up a new acquaintance quickly, and they were generally a lot smarter than people might think. Both Watson and Wolf were men she could trust.

Archie Wolf was not a fine dining aficionado. He was perfectly aware that there were those who might look upon his choice of *plat du jour* with disdain, but he just didn't give a damn. *Haute cuisine* for him was smoked, barbecued spareribs, and an establishment on South Boulevard which also boasted beer brewed on the premises was one of his favorite sources of nourishment. Thus, when Krystal accepted his invitation to dinner, he had no hesitation in selecting the venue.

In fact, Krystal was of a mind with him when it came to food. She'd grown up on a meat and potatoes diet around the kitchen table and her taste for exotic dishes extended no farther than oyster dressing with the Thanksgiving turkey. This eatery was large, but unpretentious, even utilitarian. The attraction was the quality of the food, simple and expertly prepared. She missed the taste of beer but ordered sweet tea and had to be satisfied with watching Archie enjoy the adult beverage.

As agreed between herself, Strachey, and Watson, she said nothing about assassins in the woods. Strachey reminded them that the non-disclosure agreement they signed for Whitehall was still in force. In any event, she welcomed another opportunity to talk with Archie about the Terrell case. She did not consider that Archie might have things of a more personal nature in mind.

As they both tucked into the ribs, she said, “Tell me more about Fannie Terrell’s death.”

Archie looked vaguely disappointed and chewed thoughtfully for a moment. He wiped his lips and incipient beard with his napkin and replaced the gnawed bone on his plate before answering. “Well,” he said, “this was shortly before James Terrell’s disappearance, and we can’t be sure one thing isn’t connected to the other. As I told you, I was the first officer on the scene. It was chaotic. Young Larry Terrell had discovered the body and dived into the pool to pull his sister out. They tried to resuscitate her before EMS arrived, but it was too late. It was a shame. She was a pretty young thing.”

“None of this was in the report you gave me. Why not?”

Archie shook his head. “You just asked for the report on James’s disappearance.”

“Is there anything else I should know?”

Archie ruefully regarded his cooling platter of ribs. He sighed and continued, “The mother was distraught and inconsolable. Larry had to be dragged away from the body, and then he remained at his mother's side. The kid must have been in shock. He just stood there shivering in his mother's arms staring into space. James Terrell was calm and withdrawn, just sitting in a chair at the side of the pool. Maybe he was in shock, too, but it was odd that he wasn't consoling his wife and son."

Krystal had become accustomed to Archie's archaic, in her opinion, view of sexual roles. But he was right. People react to tragedy and sudden death in different ways. Some fall apart immediately while others remain calm for a time before the full reaction sets in. Perhaps it was a delayed reaction to his daughter's death that set James Terrell off. The ones who internalize the pain tend to suffer the most.

"What do you know about Randolph Terrell," she asked.

"Oh, Randolph turned up right away. Mary had called him."

"Was he there when you arrived?"

"No. He arrived about 15 minutes later."

"What happened?"

"What do you mean?"

"What happened when Randolph arrived? What were the dynamics? Did he console his brother? Did they speak? What did he do?"

"Oh, I see what you mean. He had a few words with his brother, but James just sat there. Didn't say a word. Randolph went to help the boy and his mother. He shepherded them into the house. It seemed to me that was something James should have done. They were still in their pajamas. It was early morning. Larry was soaking wet from being in the pool. By that time the coroner had arrived." He hesitated a moment. "There was one more thing, though. The girl was completely naked. Larry had covered her body with a beach towel."

"What do you think happened? Was it suicide or accident?"

Archie took a long pull on his beer. "Hard to say. There was no note, nothing to indicate she killed herself. No signs of violence. I couldn't figure out why she was naked."

It was hard for Krystal to imagine what might have been going on in the mind of a 14-year-old suicide. Young girls are subject to all sorts of pressures and fears, imagined and real – confusion about their changing bodies, their self-image. And girls seemed so much more vulnerable than boys at that age. Had Fannie been making a statement with her nudity? No one would ever know.

"I presume the coroner pronounced it death by drowning?" asked Krystal.

"Yep. That was obvious."

"Can you get me a copy of the coroner's report?"

"I suppose so, as long as you keep it quiet."

"You know you don't have to ask," she said.

"There is another thing," he said, "something you should know about your client that may change your mind. James Terrell disappeared a week after his daughter's death. A week after that Mary Terrell had her son committed to a private mental hospital. He was there for over a year."

Her initial impression of Lawrence Terrell had been that there was something strange, a little off, about him. It had been a decade, at least, since his father's disappearance, and she knew little about what he had been doing since then. Now, she knew that at least the first year had been spent in a mental institution. Was his accusation of murder against his mother and uncle a symptom of some mental illness, or had he been committed to shut him up?

"Damn, Archie," she said. "How did I get mixed up in this?"

She was still trying to fit the pieces together as Archie drove her home. She was so distracted that she only belatedly realized that Archie had waited for a kiss, had been hoping for one, but had walked away when she had not responded to the look in his eyes. She groaned inwardly. Another complication she didn't need right now.

CHAPTER 12

The Mecklenburg County Medical Examiner and Coroner's Office is discreetly tucked away just off the Brookshire Parkway about three miles northwest of the city center. Archie Wolf's phone call to the Coroner, Dr. Stephen Barrymore, ensured that Krystal was welcomed. Not for the first time she was grateful for Archie's ready solicitude. She might not be so helpful were their positions reversed. She was not so obtuse as not to have noticed his increasing affection and was beginning to feel guilty about taking advantage of it. She was still figuring out how to respond. She liked Archie a lot, one of her few faithful friends in Charlotte, and she did not want to lose that.

Watson was with her once again. They parked in one of the spaces in the neat, small lot in front of the low, red brick building and she entered through glass doors to a cool interior where she announced herself to the receptionist.

Dr. Barrymore proved to be a genial, scholarly-looking man, slight of build, somewhere in his mid-sixties wearing gold rimmed glasses perched low on his nose, a brown tweed suit and a green tie. His carefully coiffed hair was completely white, as was his moustache. Clearly a man of the old school, he greeted her with courtly Southern politeness and escorted her down the main hallway beyond the reception area to a large office.

The office clashed with the sterile atmosphere of the building. The *décor* suggested that Barrymore had been in his position long enough to establish a comfortable, homely place to do his work. Aside from the human skeleton dangling from a tall, metal rod and the bookcases lined with medical books, this might well have been the comfortable office of a tenured university professor right down to the colorful accent rugs spread across the tiled floor.

Barrymore directed her to one of two leather-covered wing chairs set by the window on either side of an occasional table adorned with a vase of flowers. He settled himself in the other chair and said, “Sergeant Wolf asked that I give you all the help possible. What can I tell you about the Terrell case?”

“The official coroner’s report is very sparse, Dr. Barrymore,” she said. “Is there anything more you can tell me which might help with our investigation?"

Barrymore pursed his lips, removed his glasses, and cleaned them with a soft cloth he produced from his breast pocket. "It's been over ten years," he murmured, almost to himself, "and I still can't put it out of my mind. I suppose this is an appropriate time to unburden my conscience." He replaced the wire-rimmed glasses on his nose and expelled a long sigh.

"I know who you are Miss Murphy. I read the newspaper accounts of that murder case you solved. And I know who Robert Strachey is, too. His uncle and I are in the same Masonic lodge, and I respect the man a great deal." He gave her a sharp look. "May I assume that you will hold whatever I say in confidence?"

"That depends," said Krystal. "on what you say. I cannot conceal criminality, but I will try to protect you as a source."

This was not what Barrymore wanted to hear, but it was an honest response. He nodded slowly.

"I see," he said, his brow wrinkling. "I suppose that is fair. You must understand that the Terrell family is powerful and influential in Charlotte. This is an old southern city with old southern traditions, though that way of life is fading rapidly these days. And that is not all bad, mind you. That said, sensibilities and reputations are to be protected for the sake of the innocent. At least, that's the way we looked at it at the time. My examination of the poor girl's body proved beyond doubt that she died from drowning. There were no marks of violence to suggest foul play. So, it had either been accidental or a suicide. It seemed kinder to the family to call it accidental."

She sensed there was something more. "But there is something else? Something you did not put in your report?"

Barrymore stared out the window for a moment before turning back to look her in the eye. When he spoke, it was a whisper. "Yes, there was. Initially, I included it in the report, but immediately thought better of it. I destroyed that document and wrote a second one, the one you saw. There are several explanations for what I found, none of them good. Fannie was such a young girl, a beautiful girl. I did not want to inflict more pain on a family I knew well or cast a shadow over the memory of Fannie. You see, my examination showed unmistakable signs that she had had sexual intercourse only a short time before her death. I told only one person, her father, who begged me to hold this information in confidence. You see, he suspected his son, Lawrence, Fannie's twin brother. He did not want to destroy his family. You know, of course, that shortly after James disappeared, Lawrence was committed to a psychiatric facility here in Charlotte. He remained there for over a year and then was sent away to boarding school."

Krystal was shocked. "So, you believe Fannie may have committed suicide because she was having sex with her brother, that he may have raped her?"

Barrymore nodded sadly. "Given the psychiatric problems and the fact that he was sent away, that seems a reasonable explanation."

"But what about DNA testing? That could easily have identified the rapist."

"There was no DNA to test," replied Barrymore. "Her attacker must have used a prophylactic. And she had been in the water which would have washed away any other trace evidence."

"What would you have done if there had been DNA?" She was curious to see how far officials in the old south would go to protect reputations, especially moneyed reputations.

Barrymore peered at her over his glasses. "I don't know, Ms. Murphy. It would have served only to embarrass the family. I believe they did the right thing committing Lawrence to psychiatric care. As far as I'm concerned, it was the appropriate thing to do. Nothing I did or did not do would have brought the girl back."

"But how does all this relate to James Terrell's disappearance?"

"Surely, Lawrence's condition and Fannie's death created problems in the family. It may have been too much for the poor man to bear. I suspect that in the end he found some isolated place and killed himself." Barrymore shook his head sadly.

On the way back to the office her mind swirled with the facts piling on facts of this case. The death and possible rape of Fannie Terrell, the unsolved disappearance of James Terrell, and the conviction of Lawrence Terrell that Randolph and Mary had murdered James and disposed of his body. What effect had one year of psychiatric confinement had on Lawrence? Lawrence's insistence that he had seen his uncle dispose of the body. This had all the complications of a bad soap opera and no convenient resolution.

Watson dozed in the seat next to her, and Krystal was so preoccupied that she did not notice the car following her.

CHAPTER 13

It was just before noon when they returned to the office.

Ruth Scatterfield said from behind her reception desk. “Bob ordered lunch in for you. He’s waiting in his office.”

Robert Strachey was arranging cardboard containers of Chinese food on the coffee table. “Krystal, Frank, glad you’re back. Come sit down. I hope you like Chinese.”

“Who doesn’t like Chinese,” she replied scanning the assortment on the coffee table – egg rolls, mushu pork, General Tso’s chicken, rice, and some kind of vegetable dish.

Once they had divided the food, Strachey asked, “So, how did your morning go?”

“The coroner gave me some bombshell information, and I’m not sure what to do with it.”

"I'm all ears," said Robert, leaning forward.

Krystal spooned some pork onto a pancake and smothered it with hoisin sauce. "Fannie, Lawrence Terrell's twin sister who drowned in the family pool, had had sexual intercourse shortly before her death. This was a week before James Terrell disappeared."

Strachey was shocked into silence. After a long pause, he said, "That's explosive, all right. What do you make of it?"

"There is a lot to think about," began Krystal. "Was Fannie's death an accident, or did she commit suicide because she had been sexually molested? The time of her drowning is suspicious. It was the middle of the night. Was she raped earlier that same night and drowned herself out of despair or shame? She was only 14. And more pertinent to this case and us: was Lawrence having sex with his sister? He was committed to a mental hospital right after all this happened, and that's highly suggestive."

"How does all this relate to James Terrell's disappearance?" asked Strachey.

Krystal shrugged, stuffed a pork-filled pancake into her mouth and chewed for a moment. “Damned if I know. The coroner told James about Fannie but didn’t include the info in his official report. He says he wanted to spare the family a public scandal. Then James disappeared. The coroner thinks he went someplace and committed suicide, or he just ran away. There is absolutely no information I could find that would suggest what may have happened to him. Archie says there has been no new information in years.”

“Hmmm,” murmured Strachey. “There is another variant, and not a nice one. What if it was James who molested Fannie? It would explain his disappearance and suicide if that’s what happened.”

Krystal said nothing. Why do CIA guys always leap to the darkest possible explanation? She had a warm relationship with her own father and such speculation was especially repugnant to her. “That doesn’t explain why Lawrence had to be committed.”

Strachey made a sour face. “It wouldn’t be the first time for something like that. And so, James ran away, killed himself, or his wife killed him and disposed of the body? What does Archie say? What is his best guess?”

"He didn't speculate along those lines because he doesn't know about the possible rape. I think he's waiting to see what we find - fresh eyes and all that. You do things differently here in the South. Where I come from the coroner would have included everything in his report, feelings be damned."

"You need to talk to Archie again," said Strachey. "He might know if there was anything to suggest that James was a child molester."

Krystal was doubtful, and she hated the thought of presuming on Archie again. "No one I've spoken to even hinted that James was that sort of person. A ladies' man, yes, but not kids."

"Maybe," said Strachey. "But she had sex with someone shortly before her death, and she was only 14 years old. There are only two possibilities excluding some stranger who broke in and raped her."

Krystal was doubtful. "Why would Lawrence be so concerned about his father's disappearance and murder if James had been molesting his sister? It doesn't add up."

CHAPTER 14

Seated on the other side of her desk, Lawrence Terrell twitched and stared fixedly at her. She willed herself to hold his gaze despite her disgust at the thought that he may have raped his own sister.

"So, you've not found anything?" he asked, his voice laden with sarcasm, as though he didn't believe her.

Should she mention the possibility that Fannie was raped? She decided against it. There were still too many unknowns, primarily, whether the rapist was Lawrence himself.

"That's not what I said. Our very preliminary inquiries thus far have established the facts, as far as they are known. And I would not say that the circumstances aren't suspicious. That may not be news to you, but we can now share your view to a certain extent. But the case is over a decade old, and nothing new has turned up in all that time. Without some sort of lucky break, I must be honest and tell you it's unlikely we will be able to give you definite answers."

The nervous twitching stopped, and Terrell's face turned stubborn and intense. "But there could be a lucky break, couldn't there?" he insisted.

For all the fascination this case elicited, Krystal could not bring herself to like it, and the man in front of her was a big part of the reason. His presence created an unease at the base of her skull that sent little shockwaves down her spine. Nevertheless, she could not avoid feeling a certain amount of sympathy for the boy he had been and the trauma he had suffered. But what if he had raped his twin sister? Groaning inwardly, she replied, “Yes, there could be. But I can’t promise anything.”

Terrell sat there silently for a few long beats, his eyes cast down, considering what she had said. He reached a decision and locked her eyes again. “I don’t want you to stop now. I want you to continue with the investigation. There must be something.”

She was sorely tempted to tell him she could see no justification to continue the case. His best bet would be to try to forget his obsession, take advantage of the money he now had, and get on with his life. But against her best instincts, she adhered to Strachey’s insistence that they at least try. In fact, she had no idea where to go next. Despite all the intriguing clues, there was nowhere else to turn for additional information. She sat shaking her head as Terrell stalked out of the office.

She exhaled a weary, soft sigh.

CHAPTER 15

Later that afternoon, Krystal was surprised to receive a phone call at the office from Mary Terrell, who asked if it would be possible to meet with her. Doing her best to conceal her surprise, she agreed to pay her a visit mid-morning the next day.

She was becoming annoyed at Watson's insistence on accompanying her every time she stepped outside, but he would not be put off.

"Okay," she said, "but you'll get bored just sitting in the car all the time."

"I could go in with you," he said, "I'm quite a charmin' person."

"I don't think so."

She pulled up in the drive at the Terrell home, a stately brick colonial in Myers Park, at 2:00 P.M. She could imagine what Mary Terrell would say – please call off the investigation - but she was consumed by curiosity, nonetheless. Would she be confronting a once unfaithful wife who could well be a murderer, or at least an accomplice to murder? Or was this woman one of the victims? Krystal raised all her antennae in hopes of receiving strong signals one way or another.

She was met at the door by a well-kept woman in her late forties dressed more formally than the hour of the morning would dictate with an Hermès scarf drawn loosely around her shoulders and a solemn expression on her face. She must have been extremely attractive in her youth and still retained a youthful figure and an unlined face.

Mary Terrell gave Krystal an appraising look with a hint of apprehension about it and invited her in.

The Terrell home was one of the older habitations in Myers Park, at the top of a cul-de-sac, set well back, and surrounded by a large lot with old growth trees. The decor was elegant without being flashy, furnished with understated but clearly expensive modern furniture mixed with older pieces that may have been in the family for generations. Oil paintings hung on the walls, mostly of bucolic landscapes. Krystal had been around long enough to recognize the difference between old money and the nouveau riche. While the homes of the former feel lived in and comfortable, the latter tend toward the gaudy and tasteless, to the extreme of a lot of gilded furniture and glitter that reminded her of photos she had seen of

Donald Trump's living quarters in the Trump Tower in New York. The old money class does not flaunt its wealth. They are comfortable with it and wear it casually, the way you would wear a pair of old, but favorite shoes. The recently wealthy feel somehow obligated to display their good fortune in the most ostentatious, some would say vulgar, fashion.

A silver coffee service was arrayed on a low table surrounded by upholstered chairs in a sitting room at the back of the house. An empty whiskey glass sat next to the coffee, and Mary removed it to a nearby bar. The walls were lined with shelves filled with books and what must have been family photographs in silver frames. A large picture window framed an acre of mowed lawn behind the house surrounded by woods. "May I offer you some coffee?" asked Mary Terrell.

"No, thank you."

Mary gestured to a chair on one side of the table and said, "Please, sit down,." She took a seat opposite. There was a small, gilded box on the table which she opened to withdraw a cigarette. "You don't mind if I smoke?"

"Your house, your rules," said Krystal.

Mary brought the tip of the cigarette to glowing life with the flame from a silver table lighter. Her discomfort was further betrayed by a slight tremble in her hand. She held out the box to offer a cigarette to Krystal.

"No, thank you, Mrs. Terrell."

Mary took a long drag, turned her head, and blew the smoke across her shoulder from the side of her mouth. "You must excuse me," she said. "This is very difficult."

"I understand," said Krystal projecting all the sympathy she could muster. "I assume someone informed you of our investigation. That is why you called, isn't it?"

"What? Oh, yes. Agatha May Caldwell called me right after you visited her. I told my husband, and he said we should contact you immediately ... before things get out of hand."

"What do you mean?"

"You can't be that obtuse," flared Mary, finally showing some spirit as she crushed her half-smoked cigarette in an amber glass ashtray. "You must realize how such an investigation will affect our family. And when word gets out ..." she paused and shook her head from side to side. "... you have no idea how fast word of scandal spreads in this town. Sometimes it feels like a small village where everyone knows everyone else and all their secrets. We went through it after the incident ten years ago, and we don't want it to happen again. It was a horrible experience."

"Of course. I can understand your position, and we're not interested in creating a scandal. We're not seeking publicity." She could not help thinking that Mary Terrell could well be afraid of more than a mere scandal. Her phrase after the "incident" was interesting.

Mary's lips twisted into a bitter smile, and she lit another cigarette. "Well," she said, "you're off to a wonderful start. Agatha May Caldwell may be a friend, an erstwhile friend, but she's also one of the worst gossips in town. You may as well have taken out a full-page ad in the Observer."

Agatha May had not been in the least reticent talking about her friends. "I'm sorry about that, Mrs. Terrell, but it's hardly my fault."

"Oh, no? Why exactly are you doing this ... picking at old bones, I mean?" asked Mary. "Life was back to normal, and now you are asking questions, opening old wounds."

"It's what our client is paying us to do."

"You mean my son, Lawrence." She winced as she spoke his name, as if his very name caused her pain. "It can't be anyone else but him."

Krystal nodded. "Yes. He asked us to investigate his father's disappearance."

Mary Terrell's back had gone stiff, and she murmured as if speaking to herself, "We hadn't seen or heard from him in all this time. He disappeared from boarding school and just vanished. Then he turned up on our doorstep a week ago demanding his trust fund. You should not lend too much credence to what he says."

"And why is that?"

Mary hesitated a moment before speaking. "He has had ... problems, psychological problems, as I'm sure you will discover."

"You mean when he was committed?"

Mary gave her a sharp look. "You know about that?"

Krystal sensed an opening. "Do you want to talk about it?"

Mary started to speak but was interrupted by the entrance of a tall man a little older than Mary. He wore golf clothes and had a towel around his neck. "I think we've said enough already, Mary." He looked inquiringly at Krystal. "Nothing we say will change anything."

Mary averted her eyes from Krystal and said, "This is my husband, Randolph. Randolph, this is Miss Murphy. She's an investigator ..." Her voice trailed off.

Krystal assumed that Randolph had been listening to their conversation. With a tight smile that belied his stern gaze, he nodded at her. "How do you do?" He was a good-looking man with brown hair showing a lot of gray on the sides. His tanned face and arms suggested he spent a lot of time on the golf course.

"I'm pleased to meet you, Mr. Terrell. Your wife and I were about to discuss her son."

"I don't think that would be wise," he said in a neutral voice. "I think we should leave it there. I don't mean to be rude, but it's time for you to leave." He gestured toward the door.

"It might be better to talk to me now," said Krystal, but she stood, nonetheless.

"I'll show you out," said Randolph, his arm still extended toward the exit. He did not raise his voice or show any emotion, but his voice was firm.

Leaving Mary behind, they proceeded through the hall to the front door where Krystal turned and said, "You really should cooperate with me. The sooner I can finalize the investigation, the sooner it will be over. The less cooperation I get from you and your wife, the more people I must interview. It could become uncomfortable for you."

This was a thinly veiled threat, but maybe she could elicit something.

Randolph's face turned stiff with barely repressed anger. "That's a threat," he said. "The best thing for everyone would be for you to drop this ridiculous thing entirely. No good can come of it, only grief. The boy is insane, you know. He's not the sort of client you should accept."

She was inclined to agree, but said, "He doesn't seem insane to me." But he was certainly what might be termed "disturbed."

"You don't know him, and, believe me, you don't want to know him." He paused for a beat as though he had more to say. Then, "You should know that we've petitioned to have the boy committed again. His behavior towards us has been very aggressive, and my wife is frightened. The police will take him into custody as soon as we have a court order. We know where he's staying."

As she and Watson drove away, Krystal wondered if Randolph and Mary had rehearsed what they would say to her. Maybe not, to judge from Randolph's demeanor. He might have preferred to remain silent.

She was certain of one thing. There was no doubt that the Terrells were concealing something. The question which burned most brightly derived from the coroner's revelation about Fannie's autopsy. Were Randolph and Mary aware of what had happened to Fannie?

The committal came as a surprise, and she could only imagine what Lawrence Terrell's reaction would be. Was his presence so terrifying, so threatening that Randolph and Mary should take such an extreme measure? What did they hope to achieve besides silencing Lawrence?

She thought back to her last meeting with Lawrence at the PSI offices. Maybe it was the eyes, the twitchy, incongruously calloused hands with the bitten nails, the hands of a manual laborer. Whatever it was, Krystal did not like it. Clients give off vibes that she had become adept at reading. Almost all clients were nervous, at least during the initial interview. But like sonar, Lawrence broadcast signals that pinged strongly on her senses, and not in a good way.

She should take a closer look at her client. What did he do between office visits? Did he go out? Did he have friends? Legal arrangements would take some time before a commitment could take place. Should she warn him so he could hire an attorney himself? He was her client. Was she obligated to protect him?

She decided she had no such obligation. Lawrence Terrell was a disturbed young man who may well need psychiatric help.

CHAPTER 16

Randolph stood in the doorway and watched until the investigator's car entered the street and disappeared. Returning to his wife, he discovered her in tears with her face in her hands.

"What can we do?" she sobbed. "It's what we always feared after Lawrence ran away. Why did he have to come back?"

He sat on the arm of the chair and wrapped an arm around her, pulling her close, and she buried her face on his shoulder.

"We'll get through this," he said gently. "We did it once, and we can do it again."

"I'm frightened," she said. "I don't feel safe."

A spark of anger flared in Randolph. He cared deeply for his wife, and it hurt him to see her despair.

"Let's hope Dr. Dudek can get him under control again."

She stared at him with wide eyes. "Do you really think so?"

"I hope so. Lawrence was a major project for him, and he told us the treatment was successful. He'll want another go at him ... if we offer enough money."

But Randolph Terrell was worried. The images of that night ten years ago were vivid – his brother's lifeless body sprawled across his desk.

Randolph Terrell stood looking down at the body of his brother. He held a bloody hammer in his hand. The corpse was sprawled face down on the desk in James' study. There was surprisingly little blood around the wound in the back of the head and Randolph surmised that the skull had been fractured. Had the blow penetrated the skull, the released pressure would have sprayed blood all over the room. There was no doubt that James was dead.

Mary Terrell stood in the doorway sobbing with her hands over her mouth. Young Lawrence sat on the stairs outside the door in a near catatonic state. Randolph looked over at her, his face ashen. "What do you want to do, Mary?"

With some effort, she managed to bring herself under control, barely, and looked over her shoulder at Lawrence. "We can't allow anyone to know about this, Randy. We just can't."

Randoph's head was spinning with what had happened. The violence had been sudden. Such a thing had not entered his thoughts before this evening. Things had been bad enough after Fannie's death. But there would be time for regrets later. Now, he had to find a way out of the mess which could destroy his family, destroy his Mary.

He asked her to wait where she was and went to the garage where he found James' Mercedes. He put on a pair of his brother's driving gloves he found on the seat and drove to the front door. Grateful that the house sat at a considerable distance from the street, he opened the trunk and went back inside.

"Mary, please take Lawrence to his room and get him to lie down."

When they were gone, controlling a rebellious stomach, he wrapped his brother's head in clear plastic and covered it with a towel and dragged the body out the front door. He struggled to lift the heavy body into the trunk and slammed the lid shut. He had formulated an idea that might just work, but he had to act immediately.

CHAPTER 17

The impression Dr. Franz Dudek gave was a caricature of a psychiatrist. His suits were of the darker hues, he favored colorful bow ties, and his mustache and goatee were faultless. When he spoke, his voice was resonant and reassuring. The years had added girth to his frame and thinned his hair, but the extra weight only added to his gravitas. Whether it was consciously cultivated or not, behind the façade lurked a mercenary and ruthlessly ambitious character who was at the top of his game.

Right now, Dr. Dudek gazed out of the bay window in his office on the three acres of wooded land that surrounded the Wellness Psychiatric Clinic and Hospital of which he was the sole owner and manager. The boutique clinic, located at the edge of a pricey neighborhood on Charlotte's south side, represented the apex of his ambitions. He prided himself on the fact that it was the smallest and most exclusive such establishment licensed by the State of North Carolina for in-patient psychiatric care, as well as outpatient counseling. His clientèle was exclusive and unwaveringly wealthy, the sort of people who preferred discretion when it came to off-balance or excessively eccentric relatives. Such clients paid exceedingly well.

Mary and Randolph Terrell were among those well-paying clients, and he had just completed a telephone conversation with Randolph. The call reminded him unpleasantly of one of his failures. Well, not entirely a failure. He comforted himself with having achieved the primary goal of the treatments he had administered to the young Lawrence Terrell. But if the goal of the treatment was to erase certain memories, the technique had its advantages. Now, it seemed, the boy was back in Charlotte after disappearing a decade earlier. He had known the boy was still off-balance when he had released him, but all the mother wanted was a memory wiped clean. She should have been wary of the more unpleasant effects of drastic psychiatric therapy. A memory with serious gaps could leave a patient feeling disoriented and not quite whole. To be sure, the boy had not been bi-polar, the condition usually associated with electroconvulsive therapy, and so its application could not be considered entirely ethical. But it had seemed to achieve the result desired by his mother. The resulting cognitive dysfunction had been of less concern. Dr. Dudek wondered what young Terrell's current condition might be, and he had to admit that as a subject, Lawrence Terrell might still prove most interesting.

The conversation with Randolph Terrell had been disturbing. They shared a dark secret, in fact, a criminal secret. Terrell money had been sufficient to convince Dr. Dudek to discard medical ethics in the case of young Lawrence, both in accepting the task Randolph and Mary had set for him, as well as in the methodology of the treatments to which the boy had been subjected. The boy's memory was to be altered. He was to remember some facts but forget others. Unfortunately, the results were mixed.

That was a long time ago, and there had been no unwelcome consequences. Lawrence eventually disappeared, something he should have foreseen. But now he was back, and Randolph and Mary were frightened. So, they had turned once again to him to solve their problem, to make certain the events of that tragic night should never come to the surface. Dudek had insisted on knowing all the facts. He had argued that without knowing what had happened and what exactly his patient was to forget, his treatments could not be successful. This placed him in possession of information dangerous to the Terrells, but his agreement to do their bidding and the fact that he had accepted their money placed him in their power, as well. It was a situation which benefited both parties while simultaneously keeping them in check.

The opportunity to see Lawrence again after so many years, to assess the long-term results of his treatment, interested him on a purely professional level. He had never subjected a patient to the extremes the boy had endured. He was also concerned to learn how much the boy remembered of his treatment.

The Terrells knew exactly where Lawrence was staying, which simplified matters. The procedure was pretty cut and dried. He would call the police department and request official assistance in finding and apprehending Lawrence Terrell. First, of course, he would prevail upon his friend, Judge Malcolm Fitzhugh, to issue a warrant for the young man's detention and involuntary commitment to Dudek's care at the request of his mother and uncle, next of kin concerned for the young man's mental state. The fact that Lawrence had been committed before should make the judge's decision easier. Dudek wondered what the boy had been doing for the past ten years.

CHAPTER 18

Yuriy Volodin began watching the townhouse at dusk, parked in a nondescript rental car. He was a tall man, and he'd adjusted the seat as far back as it could go to accommodate his long legs. Although he did not like this assignment, the product of a madman's lust for revenge, however late, however unwise. But he would carry it to its conclusion regardless of the loss of his two colleagues. He would follow orders. It was the Russian way.

He was incredulous that the hillbilly in Georgia had taken down his two soldiers, both highly trained and experienced Department V operatives. It should have been a simple in and out operation. No fuss, no bother. They had taken the job too lightly, thinking it would be easy. The targets had seemed so ordinary, just country bumpkins. And the setting was ideal - an isolated dwelling surrounded by forest. Volodin should have done the job himself, but the long climb up that driveway would have been difficult on his gimpy leg.

Try as he might, he could not fault his planning. They had tailed the primary target for several days, determined where he lived, counted the number of people in the house. But something had gone terribly wrong. He had driven to the property, and he waited in the car to pick his men after the assignment was completed. Then came the gunfire, and he had recognized immediately that none of it came from the AR-15's his men carried. He had been around long enough to distinguish the difference between different calibers, and as soon as he heard the blast of a shotgun, he knew something had turned sour. The ensuing silence was ominous.

He beat a hasty retreat, thankful he was not followed. He promised himself he would get back to the hillbilly later. And now, miraculously, the man was here in Charlotte with the good-looking redhead.

Krystal Murphy might be a former cop, but she would not possess the capabilities to defeat the tactics Yuriy would employ. Murphy had been the prime mover in the destruction of George Wakefield's operation and the man's subsequent death, although it had been Volodin himself who had taken the shot. And for that the president of the Russian Federation deemed that she must die.

Chances were slim to none that anyone even knew he was in town. He settled down to wait and opened another pack of cigarettes. He knew they were bad for him, but he figured that with the life he had chosen it was likely that something else would kill him before the cigarettes could.

CHAPTER 19

Krystal and Watson drove straight back to the office from the Terrell home.

She went straight to Strachey. “Well, they’re having the kid committed again, and I don’t intend to warn him. It’s probably best all around. I think he’s unstable.”

“There’s nothing more we can do anyway,” said Strachey. “It would not be ethical to keep Terrell as a client if he’s judged insane.”

Krystal breathed a sigh of relief. “Gee, do you think so? You should have listened to me before. I never liked this case.”

Strachey chose to ignore the sarcasm. “We’ll have to take a step back and wait to see what happens. We’ll refund his retainer.”

“This could come back to bite us,” she said. “The Terrells have enough money to slap a lawsuit on us.”

He shook his head. “Let’s not get ahead of ourselves. We’ve done nothing wrong.”

“Then why do I feel like we did?”

“You should call Archie. Tell him we’re backing off. Fill him in on the Terrells’ plan to commit Lawrence.”

There was a clap of thunder as fat raindrops began to beat against the window.

*****

The rain was coming down, harder now. It was as if April had not given up and was battling May for supremacy. Darkness had fallen when Krystal and Watson parked in front of her townhouse. Watson was still fiddling with his seatbelt as she opened the car door and stepped out. She was tired, out of sorts, and still preoccupied with the Terrell case. And now she had no umbrella. Her cellphone rang, and she fumbled for it in her jacket pocket, cursing as it slipped through her fingers and fell to the pavement. The damned thing bounced under the car, and she bent down to retrieve it.

Which saved her life.

She heard a distinct pop, and the door window of her Audi exploded in a shower of glass just over her head. Instinctively, she dropped to her stomach on the wet pavement and slithered backwards toward the front of the car and the protection of the engine block. Looking back through the pouring rain, she saw two flashes, and bullets slammed into the front fender of her car near her head.

By now, she had drawn her Walther P99. Watson had not heard the shot, but the shattered glass alerted him. He dropped out of the passenger side door and made his way to the front of the car beside Krystal. She peeked around to where she thought the shooter was located but was unable to make out a good target. She ducked as two more rounds cut through the rear window of her Audi and out the windshield. But she had spotted a dark figure getting hurriedly into a car. She moved to her right and fired toward the windshield on the driver's side of her assailant's car, then two more at one of the headlights, which went out. She had six more .40 caliber S&W rounds left in her magazine and now Watson was firing, too. If there were two shooters, one could well be flanking them, but hunkered down as they were, they could only wait for the next shots.

She was surprised when headlights flashed on bright from the car she had been shooting at, momentarily blinding her, and allowing whoever was shooting at her a clear view. But instead of more shots, the car roared into life and rapidly backed away before executing a 180-degree maneuver in the parking lot and speeding away.

Krystal fired at the retreating vehicle before standing on wobbly legs to watch the taillights disappear into the rain. She was soaked to the skin and shaking with the sudden release of adrenaline. Watson had sprinted off to chase the escaping car but now returned, his hair and beard plastered with rain.

What the hell was that? The realization that she had been a hair's breadth from death shook her. Why had the shooter fled when he had them pinned down? Had he had been surprised when two people returned fire? She may have gotten in a lucky shot and hit the bastard. She hoped so.

Watson embraced her, lending her his warmth. "We'd better go inside," he said, his arm still around her shoulder. "Someone could still be out there."

She collected her nerves hoping there was no one else out in the darkness before holstering her pistol and moving back to the side of her car. She stooped and found her cellphone in a puddle. "Thanks, phone. You saved my life."

She had to call the cops, but they must get out of the open first. Sirens already were sounding, getting closer. Neighbors must have reported the gunshots.

His head swiveling in all directions, Watson preceded her into the house, gun in hand. She followed, and they meticulously cleared each room before she dialed Archie Wolf's cellphone number. It was nearly 11 P.M., but he answered on the third ring. "Wolf. Is that you, Krystal?"

"Yeah, it's me. Listen, something has happened ..."

"What's going on?"

"Well, someone just tried to kill me."

"What? Jesus! Where are you? Are you still in danger?"

"I don't know. About the danger, I mean. I don't think so. I'm at home, and I hear sirens."

"But are you safe now?"

"Yeah, I'm OK, and Frank Watson is with me. Just tell me when you get here, and I'll let you in. There are cops on their way already. I hear sirens."

"Hang tight. I'll be there in ten minutes."

She had to call Strachey. If it had been one of Watson's Russians who attacked her, it meant they were already in Charlotte and on the hunt.

"Damn it, Krystal! Are you OK? Are you safe now?" Strachey asked. "I'll be right there."

"No need, Bob. I'm inside my house, Frank is here, the cops are on their way, and I called Archie Wolf. We can talk about everything at the office tomorrow morning. This is not over, and it's something we're all going to have to face together."

"What will you tell Archie?"

"I hate to do it, Bob, but we should talk it over before we say anything to the police about the Wakefield thing. We should ask Whitehall."

Strachey did not reply immediately, and when he did, he did not sound happy. "OK, play it by ear for now. And for God's sake, be careful."

"I will."

She collapsed onto the sofa as the adrenaline drained from her system, and her body reacted to what had happened. Prudence dictated that she not turn on the lights until Archie arrived, and she sat in the darkness listening to the sound of her own heart and the clink of ice in a glass. Watson had discovered the bottle of scotch under her kitchen sink. She realized that her hands were shaking and that she was wet and cold and that her sofa must be soaked. Scotch sounded good.

She was tempted, but decided against a drink.

Sirens sounded outside, and there was a flash of red and blue on her curtains to announce the arrival of the police. She was already on her way to the door when there was a knock, and she opened it to greet two uniformed cops on her stoop. The parking lot was bathed in the flashing lights of three police cars. Several cops were searching the area with flashlights, and another was examining the bullet holes in her Audi.

The rain had slackened, but there was a rumble of thunder in the distance threatening a resumption of the downpour.

She was pointing out the damage to her car when Archie arrived in his jeep. He leapt out and trotted quickly over to her with concern written all over his face. He wore jeans and a black hoodie. “Are you OK, Krystal? What the hell happened?” His eyes were wide with alarm, and he would have embraced her, but she stepped back out of his reach. “I’m all wet,

Archie." She did not want to be touched right now.

She felt unaccountably embarrassed that Archie should see her in this state, sopping wet, her hair plastered to her head. She gave an account of the attack, and he asked, "Do you have any idea who might have been shooting at you?"

He unfolded an umbrella and held it awkwardly over her head.

A van with Charlotte-Mecklenburg police markings joined the other police vehicles. Glancing over his shoulder, Archie said, "That will be the CSU," and repeated his question. "Who did this?"

"I can't be sure," she said with a shake of her head. "I'll have to think about it, and we can talk tomorrow when my head is clearer. Right now, I'm wet and cold, and all I want is a hot shower and a dry bed."

She hated withholding information from Archie, but there were a lot of things to consider, including FBI involvement. She soothed her conscience with the thought that there was plenty of time to sort things out. Right now, she needed to calm down and get her head straight.

But Archie wasn't giving up. "Could this have anything to do with the Terrell case? You've been digging up some old bones, Krystal. Could it have been Randolph Terrell trying to shut you down?

"Uh, I don't think so." In fact, the thought had not occurred to her. But now that Archie mentioned it, the idea was not entirely out of the question – if the Terrells had something to hide, and from all appearances, they did ... At least, it was an idea which made it possible to avoid mentioning Russians.

"Then who the hell was shooting at you?"

She bit her lip. "You may be right about Terrell, but I'll have to think about it, Archie. There are a couple of possibilities."

She immediately regretted her words.

He gave her a sharp look. "Really? Do you have that kind of enemy, and more than one? Here in Charlotte?"

"I've been around the block a few times, Archie." It was a weak response, but it was all she had.

He was not satisfied with her answer. After a beat, he said, "OK, Krystal. We'll talk tomorrow first thing. I'll post a guard out here for the night. If you like, I can get a female police officer to stay in the house with you."

"Thanks, Archie, but that's not necessary. I'm fine, really. Right now, I just want a hot shower and some dry clothes. And Frank Watson is still here."

She provided an account of what had happened as the cops searched the parking area for shell casings and other evidence.

She left him standing in the rain and went back inside and headed for the bathroom where she stripped off the soaking clothes and ran the shower as hot as she could stand it. She stood under the steaming water for a long time trying to clear her head and exorcise the tension from her body.

CHAPTER 20

Yuriy Volodin was shocked. It was not the first time he had been shot, but he had not expected immediate and accurate return fire from the woman. He had ducked back into the car after his first shots missed with the intention of escaping, but one of her bullets came through the windshield and struck his left shoulder. There had been no pain at first, only numbness, but he knew the pain would come soon. It felt like his clavicle was shattered.

He sped away from the townhouse complex, fighting to remain conscious as the pain seared his shoulder and sent shock waves coursing through his body. By now his shirt and jacket were drenched with blood. He had to staunch the flow. But where could he seek medical attention for a gunshot wound? He was in a foreign city on a clandestine mission for his government.

He could feel the energy draining from him and his vision blurred. He slowed, taking his foot off the gas pedal, and the car drifted to the right, bumped over the curb, and came to a stop against a telephone pole.

He had just enough strength left to make a call on his cellphone.

He had no idea how long he had been there as a kind of twilight engulfed him. Then there were voices followed by flashing lights. People put their hands on him and lifted him from the car.

Off to the side, a thin man with a beard and narrow nose glared at him with burning eyes.

And that was all he knew until he regained consciousness with no idea of how much time had passed. There was sunlight coming through a window somewhere. Obviously, several hours had passed. He was lying prone in a bed with beeping and blinking instruments all around him.

He tried to raise his head but fell back onto the pillow as a wave of nausea swept over him. He recognized the dryness in his mouth as a sign that he had been drugged.

His left shoulder was heavily bandaged with his arm immobilized across his chest. He right wrist, ne noticed, was shackled to the bed with a handcuff.

Why hadn't he employed a rifle in the attack on the woman? He was much more proficient with a long gun than a pistol, but he had been overconfident. And the woman had ducked to the ground just as he fired, a freakish stroke of luck for her. Otherwise, she would be dead, and he could turn his attention to the other target.

For the time being, there was nothing he could do. He would have to await a chance to escape.

CHAPTER 21

Krystal opened her eyes to the morning light invading her bedroom in horizontal rays through the venetian blinds. She stretched lazily and then shot straight up as the memory of the night before flooded back. She was surprised to see the time was 7:30 A.M., an hour and a half later than her normal wake-up time, a habit that had stuck with her from farm life in Indiana.

Last night's rain had passed, and the morning promised a warm day. She caught the aroma of bacon and coffee as she came down the stairs and found Watson in the kitchen preparing breakfast. He had his long hair tied behind his head and wore jeans and a checked cotton shirt.

"We best get a good breakfast inside us, Red. I have a feelin' it's goin' to be a long day."

She looked out the window half expecting to see Archie Wolf's jeep parked in front of her door. It would be so like the man to see personally to her safety. She was slightly disappointed to see only a police squad car.

Watson watched her as he tended to the the skillet on the stove. "If you're lookin' for your buddy Archie, he left a couple of hours ago. You got somethin' goin' on with that guy, Red?"

She turned from the window, embarrassed by Watson's perceptive question.

"No," she said quickly, "Not really." Frankly, she didn't know how to respond. Was 'something going on' between her and Archie? Her thoughts were too scrambled to contemplate that question right now.

"Um hum." Watson spooned scrambled eggs onto their plates next to toast and bacon and poured black coffee into their cups.

"It might not have been the Russians," she said, anxious to change the subject. "Last night, Archie suggested it could have been Randolph Terrell taking potshots at me. He could have a motive to put an end to the investigation, so it's not entirely out of the question. We don't know for sure that it was some Russian hitman."

"I don't think so," he said. "When Archie came back last night, he was pleased as punch. Seems like one of us plugged the bastard what did the shootin,' and he passed out in his car. They took him to the hospital to be patched up, so he's in custody."

She stared at him, wide-eyed. "Why the hell didn't you tell me that first? It changes everything."

"Maybe," drawled Watson as he hoisted a forkful of scrambled egg. "It was a pretty darned well-planned ambush. You came real close to buyin' it last night."

It was an uncomfortable thought, but he was right. That first shot would have taken her head off had she not stooped to pick up her phone. "We'll talk it out with Bob this morning."

"What about your friend?" He pronounced it "freeyend" loaded with mischievous innuendo. "What are you gonna tell him about the Roosians?"

She bit her lip. "I don't know." Sometimes she could just smack Watson in the face.

Watson picked a rasher of bacon off his plate with his fingers and bit off a piece. "I have a feelin' that feller is gonna be very curious."

"Yep. He will."

Breakfast finished, she retreated upstairs to avoid any more conversation about Archie. She brushed her teeth and spritzed on a dash of perfume before coming back down, grabbing a light jacket and heading for the door.

Her Audi was nowhere in sight. "Where is my car?"

"CSU took it last night. So, you'll have to ride with me," said Watson, nodding toward his Harley.

She was still thinking about Archie Wolf. "You say Archie remained out here most of the night, but then left?"

The cop got out of his car and stepped toward them. "Sergeant Wolf wants to see you at police headquarters this morning."

Not before they planned what to say and coordinated their story.

To the cop: "Sure. No problem. Tell the Sergeant to call me to set something up."

She couldn't very well avoid reporting to the police altogether. The more she resisted, the more suspicious they would be. It was not such a bad idea to bring Archie into the picture regardless of the non-disclosure agreement with the FBI. He had proven his worth and discretion several times. In fact, he had never protested when she asked for some off-the-books help or a peek into police files. He had even plugged her in with the county coroner a few days ago. Yes, she owed him some trust and courtesy. And more importantly, he could keep a secret. They would need his cooperation with the Charlotte Mecklenburg Police.

After thanking the cop, she turned to Watson who was holding a motorcycle helmet out to her. *Shit. There goes my hair.* She was glad she wore jeans today.

Twenty minutes later, they found Strachey sipping a mug of steaming coffee in his office. He was dressed casually in jeans and a light cotton pullover. He gestured for them to take seats. “You guys want some java?”

Watson asked for a cup of black American coffee, but Krystal demurred. “Bob,” she said, “I think we should brief Archie on what’s really going on. The cops have the shooter from last night in custody.”

Strachey arched his eyebrows as he twiddled with the controls on the coffee machine.

“It’s likely we’ll need his help,” she persisted. “He’ll be a fourth arrow in our quiver.”

“He may be too straight an arrow for this,” said Strachey. He handed Watson a cup of coffee.

She was about to speak when her cellphone chimed. Caller ID told her it was Archie Wolf.

"Hi, Archie," she began, then stopped, listening, and could not disguise her surprise. "Er, thanks, Archie. Listen, we need to talk. Can you stop by the office right away?"

She listened for a moment, then: "No, Archie, it's really important, and we need to discuss it before we talk to your guys."

She put the phone away and turned to the others who were looking at her curiously. "He confirmed they have last night's shooter," she said, her voice flat. "He was admitted to hospital early this morning with a gunshot wound to the shoulder and admitted to surgery."

"How do they know it was your shooter?" asked Strachey.

"For one thing, his car was full of bullet holes, and he was less than a mile from my place."

"Is he a Russian?"

"They don't know. He has an American ID, but Archie thinks it's phony. And he speaks English with a definite accent. I didn't want to mention the Russian possibility on the phone."

"If it's our man, it's a helluva big break for us. So, Archie spoke with him?" asked Strachey.

She nodded. "He was at the hospital when the guy woke up this morning. They have him under guard. According to Archie, he wasn't very talkative."

"If he's a Vympel operative, they'd better double the guard," said Strachey. "Is Archie coming to see us?"

"He's on his way now. He sounded grim."

"Well," said Strachey, "he's going to be even grimmer when he finds out what this is all about."

CHAPTER 22

Archie arrived looking haggard and bleary-eyed from lack of sleep.

Strachey greeted him. “You look like a man who could use some coffee.”

Archie wanted “regular American black coffee,” which won him an approving nod from Watson. The cop sank heavily into one of the leather chairs in the corner. “We got the bastard,” he said, his voice heavy with fatigue. “He’s a scary looking guy, and I wonder how the hell you managed to make an enemy of him.”

The question was directed at Krystal.

Strachey busied himself with the steam punk coffee machine at his wet bar, adjusting the knobs to brew American style coffee while Krystal fetched a white Navy mug from the cupboard for Archie. The coffee machine, with its copper and brass fittings looked like something out of an H.G. Wells novel.

When they all were settled around the coffee table, Strachey finally lit his morning cigar. “OK, Krystal, so why don’t you fill Archie in? Then we can discuss next steps.” She was grateful he didn’t question her decision.

"Next steps?" asked Archie.

"You need to hear this," said Strachey.

Krystal told the story of how she and Watson had first encountered former CIA mucketymuck George Wakefield during a murder investigation. They had eventually uncovered a conspiracy between Wakefield and Russian intelligence to mount a vast influence operation in Washington targeting members of Congress, among others. In the end, Wakefield had captured Krystal and Watson and was on the verge of killing them when Strachey arrived with the cavalry in the form of the FBI Hostage Rescue Team. Another player had been the FBI's legendary and mysterious counterintelligence guru, Enoch Whitehall. They still did not know who had shot and killed Wakefield.

"And then there was the attack on Frank," she concluded.

Archie turned to Watson. "What attack."

"Some fellers snuck up to my house with the idea of murdering my family and me. They didn't make it far." Watson gave a condensed version of what happened in Georgia. "That's why I came up here. The FBI thought it was a good idea," he added.

Krystal said, “And now we think the guy you have in the hospital may be a Russian assassin, a pro.”

Strachey added, “I think we’re dealing with a Moscow-trained thug, probably ex-Spetsnaz. Maybe the GRU’s Unit 29155, maybe Alfa Group or the FSB’s Department V. If I’m right, we’re dealing with the best they have.”

“Crap,” said Archie. “He refused to say a word to me, but he’s weak and drugged up. This is big and it’s complicated.”

“The FBI kept the darker stuff about Wakefield under wraps,” Strachey explained. “That information was just too explosive to be made public, especially at a time when confidence in the government is at an all-time low. Several congressmen were quietly informed that they would not be running for office again. It was a big deal. You understand, Archie, that none of his information can leave this office. It’s a national security matter.”

Archie took a sip of coffee and made a face when he discovered it had gone cold. He replaced the mug on the table. “I understand,” he said, “I was in the military. But it’s going to be hard to explain last night and the guy we have in the hospital to Curry without letting him in on the secret stuff."

Strachey shook his head. "Curry can't know," he said, "at least for the time being. It's not our decision to make. We may already be in trouble with the FBI for briefing you into the case." He shot a glance at Krystal. He drew on his cigar and discovered it had gone out. He walked to his desk and retrieved his lighter before continuing.

"I called Enoch Whitehall this morning. He is the ultimate authority on the classified nature of all this. When I told him about the attempt on Krystal's life, he said he would send someone down here. I didn't know that the shooter was in custody. He also insisted we were to reveal nothing about the Wakefield connection. It's still a matter of national security according to him, and any mention of it will bring the press sniffing around. The media are still curious about the Wakefield matter. So, Archie, we have no choice for the time being but to keep this information from the police. I know this puts you in a difficult position, but the decision has been taken away from us by Whitehall. The best thing is to act for the time being as if the shooter is unidentified and pursue a routine investigation. That should satisfy Curry for the time being. If anything goes wrong, the blame can be laid on the FBI's doorstep."

Archie still looked dubious. "I find it difficult to have a lot of faith in the FBI these days."

"We don't have any choice in the matter, Archie," said Strachey.

"I don't like it," insisted Archie, "especially when politics are involved."

"We have no choice," repeated Strachey. "And I trust Whitehall."

"When is the FBI guy due?" asked Krystal.

"He should fly in later today. He'll come straight here. He obviously doesn't yet know the shooter is in custody."

"I think Archie should be here, too," she continued. "It's only fair. And, Archie, there may be a lot wrong with the FBI these days, but I have a lot of faith in Enoch Whitehall."

Whitehall had been kind to her when she was still a cop in Arlington. More than once he had taken her under his wing and set her in the right direction.

His antecedents were a mystery, but he he wielded considerable power in Washington.

Archie looked at the floor, not a happy camper.

CHAPTER 23

Archie Wolf left with conflicting thoughts in which Krystal Murphy figured prominently.

He knew he was not an especially attractive man. He was lanky in a backwoods sort of way, and his accent was purely hill country, which he did not try to hide. Rather than the chiseled jaw and broad brow of action heroes, his face was narrow with sharp features. These physical characteristics could lead people to underestimate him, and that, combined with razor sharp intelligence that could be seen if one looked into his Arctic blue eyes, was an advantage which had stood him in good stead in his professional life.

From the first he had sensed a kindred spirit in the auburn-haired Yankee cop who had walked into his life a year and a half ago. He admired her professional competence and independent spirit which some mistook for obstinance. He had gone out of his way to cooperate with her on a professional level, more than once breaking the rules to do so. And he had to admit there had been an element of personal motivation in that.

He knew she had been serious about someone when they met, but something had changed. She confided nothing in him, but he sensed that she had been hurt. When that happened, people erected barriers against intimacy.

Now, this vendetta-bound killer from her past had attacked her. I mean, what the hell kind of shit had she gotten herself into? The FBI? State secrets? This sort of thing was new to him, and it made him extremely uncomfortable. He knew police procedure, and this was not it. Curry would be anxious to know the reason for the attack and what was known about the man in the hospital, and he had every right to know. But now Archie was under some sort of prohibition against doing his duty? Still, Krystal had demonstrated that she trusted him by bringing him into the secret, a mixed blessing, for sure. She had not batted an eye while discussing an assassin who had targeted her, as if such events were commonplace.

There was no putting off Curry, who insisted on meeting Krystal that afternoon, and he was uncomfortably nervous when he escorted her into his boss's office.

Captain Abel Curry rose to his full 6'1" height when they entered. Whether this was gentlemanly courtesy to a woman or intended to intimidate was hard to tell.

"Let's sit over at the table," he said in his smoker's voice. He was a big man in his 50's with a shaved head and heavy five o'clock shadow, the perfect type to play the villain in any movie. The odor of cigarette smoke hung in the air despite the prohibition against smoking in public buildings.

They took their places around a scarred, wooden conference table blotched with rings left by innumerable coffee cups and glasses. There were cigarette burns, as well, despite the large ashtray defiantly placed in its center.

Curry wore a slightly wrinkled dark blue suit, and his tie was loosened. "Well, Miz Murphy," he began. "You had a little trouble at home last night. Care to tell me what happened?"

As Archie squirmed a bit in his seat, Krystal gave a forthright account of the events of the previous evening.

Curry remained unreadable. "Do you have any idea who it was who attacked you?"

Krystal's stomach gave a little somersault as she began to speak. She didn't like lying to the police, even less so to Abel Curry. She could be putting Archie's job in jeopardy, as well as ruining her own reputation with the police. She was at the very least taking advantage of Archie's affection for her. "Er, not really," she said. "I'm working on an investigation right now which might have prompted such a reaction. But nothing is certain at this point."

"Um hum." Curry fiddled with a scarred Zippo cigarette lighter he pulled from his pocket. "And what investigation might that be?"

"We've been retained to investigate the disappearance of James Terrell. His family is quite upset that we are resurrecting the case."

Curry either could not or cared not to conceal his surprise. "James Terrell? We have a file on that, don't we, Archie? Cold case?"

"Yes," replied Archie. "Terrell disappeared without a trace over a decade ago. His wife and brother were suspected, but nothing could be proved."

Curry nodded. "Yes, I remember. And have we been helping Miz Murphy with her investigation?" His tone was deceptively quiet - a danger signal.

Archie managed a straight face. "I briefed her on what happened at the time."

Krystal was impressed by his *sang froid.* Before the meeting, she and Archie agreed to provide a truthful but bare bones account of last night's attack and no more. They would not outright lie to Curry, but they would go no further.

"Hummph," Curry grunted, conveying his suspicion that Archie had been more than generous with the information provided to the auburn-haired detective. "Despite our genteel past and appearances, Miz Murphy, Charlotte has become a dangerous city. We rank in the lower five percent in terms of crime. Could your incident just be an armed robbery attempt gone wrong?"

"Er, I don't think so," said Krystal. "Whoever it was just started shooting with no warning."

Curry flipped open his lighter and snapped it closed. "You shot back. Apparently, you wounded your assailant."

Archie jumped in. "That's what we think. Not only does the guy have a bullet wound in his shoulder, but his car has some holes, too."

"Yes, well, you were lucky," said Curry. "Thanks for coming in, Miz Murphy. We'll be in touch if we learn anything from this guy. Someone must have hired him unless he has something personal against you himself. Can you think of anyone like that?"

"Not off-hand," she replied.

Curry sighed. "Our murder rate is the highest it's been in decades, and it's not really getting any better. This won't help the statistics."

Curry paused for a beat. He fastened his eyes on her. "What have you folks at PSI been up to that could have brought this on?"

She willed herself to conceal her discomfort. "PSI has not been involved in anything other than normal security and investigation jobs." The absolute truth.

"Uh huh." Curry didn't sound convinced. "That partner of yours is ex-CIA, isn't he? Could something out of his past be behind this?"

The captain was getting uncomfortably close to the truth. "I suppose that's possible," she said carefully. "But you would have to talk to him."

"Maybe I'll do that," said Curry.

He shifted his gaze to Archie. "See what you can find out from the shooter. I want to know exactly who he is and whether someone hired him."

"Sure thing, Captain," said Archie.

Curry stood up, and they followed suit.

"Thanks again, Miz Murphy, I'm sorry for your trouble. Please be careful."

"Thank you, Captain Curry. I certainly will."

They walked out to the parking lot where Watson waited with his Harley.

"That was good, Archie," she said.

"I still don't like it," he frowned. "Curry is no dummy, and he asked about Strachey."

"We didn't lie to him. In fact, we don't know any more than what we told him. All this other stuff is still only speculation."

"Strachey and your buddy Watson don't seem to think it's speculation. What happens if the shit hits the fan? What do we tell Curry then?"

"We'll have to cross that bridge when we come to it."

CHAPTER 24

Is there a difference between revenge and retribution? Lawrence sometimes thought about this question. He decided that retribution was the more honorable because he saw it as righting a wrong, whereas mere revenge could be exacted for either a right or a wrong act. His reasoning was not exact, but it satisfied him. Retribution was his game.

He remembered two bodies. One was that of his father, his head bludgeoned. He remembered watching as the body was loaded into the trunk of a car. The car had disappeared into the night, and he remembered nothing after that until he emerged as if from a thick fog in that place they sent him. The second body was that of his sister - wet, naked, a stream of water running from her hair, cold onto his arm as he carried her from the pool behind the family home. He had loved his sister beyond words, and now she was dead, her face glistening in the moonlight inches from his, her eyes empty, staring up at him as if asking why he let this happen. The rest swirled unseen in a black mist he could not penetrate. These two facts were all he had, the beginning and end of his memories of home. He spent years trying to divine their meaning and finally had convinced himself that there was only one explanation. And retribution was required.

This left Lawrence Terrell perilously suspended between rage and euphoria. The simmering rage had long ago burrowed deeply into his soul. For over a decade its roots had extended themselves to undergird his every thought, his every action. That rage had inspired him to commit acts which most would deem unspeakable, but they made it possible for him to survive. He was too clever by far ever to be caught, and he rationalized what he had done by telling himself it was all preparation for one final act which would right all the wrongs inflicted upon him and his sister.

Rage carried him through the years of exile. His mother and his uncle had sent him away, interred him in a place he could not escape, a place of words, needles, pills, and worse. He was unsure of how long he had spent there, but eventually they released him. And then they sent him to a boarding school in Connecticut, far from his home in Charlotte. Obviously, they wanted him as far away as possible because they feared him, feared what he knew and what he might say. Of this he was convinced.

The boarding school had not held him for long. One night he had packed a bag and crept off the campus. That had been ten years ago, and he had drifted ever since, working hand to mouth, occasionally stealing, living in homeless shelters or public housing. But he had not forgotten the trust fund his father had set up at his birth. The money would provide him with a new, wider freedom than he had yet known.

Now, the police had seized him, putting his plan in danger. His wrists hurt where the cuffs dug into them behind his back. The back seat of the police cruiser stank of a mixture of antiseptic, piss, and puke. Lawrence's initial fright was supplanted by anger, like the darkness before a thunderstorm. This was not right, not fair. His ire deepened when he saw where he was being taken. The red brick building in the wooded setting was frighteningly familiar, a place of pain and horror that haunted his nightmares and stirred his resentment to smoldering rage.

The police led him into the building where two muscular, white-clad attendants waited. The cops removed the cuffs and left after having some papers signed by a woman behind a reception desk. The attendants each took an arm and led him down a long hallway to an office door. They knocked, and a voice from the past struck his ears like a blow.

Lawrence's memories of the building were muddled, but they were united by a general sense of dread and memories of pure terror. And that dread was associated with the reedy voice of Dr. Franz Dudek. Lawrence trembled as the attendants led him into the doctor's office, and the fear made him even more desperate.

"Should we remain, doctor?" asked one of the attendants.

Dudek did not rise from behind his desk. He looked up from what he had been reading and regarded Lawrence with an avuncular smile. "My boy," he said, spreading his arms wide. "Won't you take a seat?" He gestured to a chair in front of the desk, and the attendants pushed Lawrence down into it, their heavy hands resting on his shoulders.

Dudek remembered Lawrence as a frail, frightened and confused boy of 14, harmless and easily coerced. He had controlled the boy completely, bent him to his will, changed his very memories. And this gave the psychiatrist confidence he should not have had.

Lawrence remained silent and still, his eyes fixed on the doctor, who blithely waved the attendants out of his office. “You can wait outside,” he told them. “Lawrence and I are old friends.”

In a few moments, those words would ring hollow.

When they were alone, Dudek, using his most soothing voice, said, “Lawrence, I am sorry to see you back at the clinic, but I’m certain we will be able to work through whatever seems to be bothering you. Just like before.”

Unfortunately for Dudek, Lawrence was no longer the malleable boy he had been. Over a decade scraping by on the street had hardened him. He had been hungry and stolen food. He had been beaten until he had grown strong enough to fight back. And his anger had made him even stronger.

His eyes landed on an obsidian paperweight in the form of an Aztec god on Dudek’s desk. In an instant he surged from the chair, grabbed the paperweight, and leapt across the desk as Dudek squealed like a pig and raised his arms in a futile attempt to protect himself.

Lawrence easily overcame the portly psychiatrist and smashed the heavy paperweight into the side of his head before he could make another sound.

Lawrence felt like he was slaying a fire-breathing dragon which had once imprisoned him in a deep hole. Dudek was evil, a torturer, a bender of minds, a slayer of memories. Lawrence had escaped his clutches once, but now the torturer had found him again, had snatched him off the street and dragged him back to his dark keep. But Lawrence was cleverer now and emboldened by desperation. He would kill Dudek and be rid of his shadow forever.

Dudek was stunned, barely conscious and groaning. Lawrence struck him again and would have done more, but he did not know whether anyone had heard the doctor's high-pitched cries or when the orderlies might come through the door again. Dudek had screamed, but lay motionless now, blood streaming from his head.

There was little time to lose. He rose from Dudek's body and turned to the French doors. The doctor's office was on the ground floor. Outside the French doors was a large flower bed and a narrow strip of lawn bordered by a wooded area.

Lawrence slipped outside, looked both ways and ran into the trees.

Everyone in his life had betrayed him, including the auburn-haired detective who kept telling him there was nothing to be done to bring justice to his father's murderers. She had had her chance and failed. Now it was his turn to make things right. In his pocket was a ring of keys he had carried since running away. He hoped his mother and uncle had not changed the locks on the house in Myers Park.

CHAPTER 25

A Citation V private jet landed at Charlotte/Douglas International Airport. The lone passenger disembarked and entered a black limousine waiting on the tarmac. An hour later, he arrived at PSI. A wide-eyed Ruth Scatterfield escorted him to Strachey's office where he, Krystal, Watson, and Archie Wolf had gathered.

As soon as the familiar gaunt figure, dressed in a tailored charcoal suit, white shirt, and black tie appeared in the doorway, Krystal leapt to her feet. "Director Whitehall!"

If she expected a warm greeting from him, she was disappointed.

Whitehall paused in the doorway for a moment as he took in the scene. He recognized Krystal, Strachey, and Watson, but his stare fixed on Archie Wolf who felt some discomfort as those dark grey eyes calmly inspected him.

The FBI's Executive Assistant Director for Counterintelligence was tall, almost cadaverous, with deep set gray eyes set in a hatchet face on either side of a long blade of a nose. His thinning hair was white and swept straight back in a style that would have been familiar in the 1930's. His attention focused on Archie, he asked, "Who is this?"

The voice was neutral and distant. If there was any displeasure, it was hard to detect. He turned to Krystal.

"Erm, Director Whitehall, this is sergeant Archie Wolf of the Charlotte Mecklenburg Police. We," she glanced at the others for support, "thought it necessary to brief him on the Russian case."

As though Archie wasn't there, Whitehall asked, "Is he trustworthy?"

Archie started to rise, but Strachey laid a restraining hand on his arm.

"Yes, sir," said Krystal. "You can have full confidence in him and in his discretion."

"Nevertheless," continued Whitehall, "his presence is an unwelcome surprise. As I recall, I impressed upon the three of you the need for secrecy the last time we met in my office."

There was an awkward silence finally broken by Strachey, "We didn't feel we had a choice. A gun battle in a quiet neighborhood does attract police attention. And we need Archie's support.

Please, have a seat, Mr. Whitehall. May I offer you some coffee?"

Ignoring Strachey's offer, Whitehall stood for a moment in silence. "He'll have to sign a non-disclosure agreement," he said at last. "No coffee, thank you, Mr. Strachey. I won't be here long, and I want to make the most of the time. I'm flying back to Washington later this morning." He took a seat.

"The situation is grave," he continued. "I was distressed to learn of the attempt on your life, Krystal, though not surprised. I suspected there would be more trouble after what happened to Mr. Watson and his family. What surprised me was that you had not taken precautions before there was an attempt on your own life."

Krystal choked back an indignant response. Damn it, Whitehall was right. She had been forewarned. She should have been more alert.

Archie spoke up. "I never heard of the Russians attempting an assassination on U.S. soil. Is this something new?"

"No," Whitehall replied, "The Russians attempted an assassination back in 2020 in Florida. The target was the defector, Aleksandr Poteyev who provided information leading to unmasking a

Russian illegals network. In that instance, the Russians, the GRU, adopted a more discrete approach. Now, they have opted to be more direct.

"The question," he continued, "is what to do next. Obviously, we cannot just wait for the assassin to strike again or hope that he just goes away. That would cede the advantage to him. We must seize the initiative. Do you have any ideas, Mr. Strachey? For reasons that should be obvious, I would prefer not to widen the circle of knowledge unless absolutely necessary. With your background, Mr. Strachey, I would expect you to have some ideas about how to handle the situation. You have four very capable people, including yourself, to work with."

Strachey managed to conceal the satisfaction he felt in surprising Whitehall. "We have the perpetrator already, Director Whitehall. He's under police custody in the hospital with a bullet wound, thanks to Krystal's good aim."

The normally phlegmatic Whitehall only widened his eyes slightly as he digested the information. After a pause, he asked, "I assume a police report already has been filed. Is there any reference to him being a

Russian?" The question was directed at Archie.

"No ... sir. We have no evidence concerning the perp's nationality." Archie was not developing warm feelings for Whitehall. Normally in such a case, the police would welcome FBI involvement, but Whitehall was a horse of a different color, someone who felt he didn't have to play by the rules.

"Well, well," murmured Whitehall. "That, at least, is encouraging. You may have saved all of us a lot of trouble, Sergeant Wolf. How serious are his injuries? Is he expected to survive?"

"The bullet struck him in the shoulder and shattered his clavicle. But his life is not in danger."

"Well," said Whitehall, "that's not ideal, but we'll just have to work with it."

Archie sat up. "What do you mean? We have him in custody. He's not going anywhere, and we already have enough evidence to file charges."

Whitehall was unaccustomed to having to explain himself, and with a cold look at Archie said, "This is not a normal police matter, sergeant. It is a matter of national security, which means it cannot be left to local authorities. The Bureau will be handling things from now on."

This time, Strachey could not restrain Archie who sprang to his feet. "What does that mean? We already have the case in hand. What am I supposed to tell my boss?" He shot a reproachful look at Krystal who only shook her head. She had considerable experience with Director Whitehall which had engendered considerable respect. The man had come through for her more than once and had even saved her life.

Whitehall regarded Archie with what might have been mild amusement or mild annoyance, and he injected some authority into his voice. "That is nothing you should concern yourself about, sergeant. Your department will know only that the FBI has assumed control of the case. Period. No further explanation is necessary. You and your colleagues might not like it, but that is the way it will be." He paused for a beat, then: "And you will be sworn to secrecy. It would have been better if your friends here had not filled you in on the case."

Still seething, Archie turned to Strachey. "So, you really believe this is some kind of Russian intel operation … here in the States?"

Strachey nodded, "Recent Russian assassinations have been more subtle than simply shooting at the target. They've incorporated radioactive substances, poison, and even third country nationals as in the Florida case Director Whitehall mentioned where they used a Mexican doctor. I suspect that what we're dealing with here is a Spetsnaz soldier seconded to the FSB, most likely a Vympel type. He's had some intel training, but he's not an intel officer."

"What the hell is 'Vympel?'" Archie asked.

The use of the arcane terminology of espionage was normal to Strachey, and he sometimes forgot that most people lacked his experience. "Vympel," he replied, "means 'banner." It's the name of a special paramilitary operations group established in the KGB's First Chief Directorate in the early 80's. The group is now part of the FSB."

Krystal rolled her eyes. The last thing she wanted to hear right now was a lecture on the esoteric practices of the KGB.

"Strange name they chose," grumbled Archie. "But it's just speculation. It seems to me you're taking a lot for granted."

"There's no other choice, Archie," said Krystal. She noticed that Whitehall was studying Archie in a manner not unlike a mongoose studying a cobra. Something like this was well outside Archie's experience. He was a cop used to procedure. She could only imagine what was going through his mind.

Archie turned back to Whitehall. "What do you plan to do with this guy? No due process? Just make him disappear?"

Whitehall said, "This is not a police matter, Sergeant Wolf. We are far beyond the normal bounds of law and order. Normally, I would favor an arrest and trial, but in this instance, we must act extra-judicially and err in favor of keeping information out of the public realm. Anything regarding the Wakefield affair is verboten. That is the diktat of the powers that be. It must be kept entirely off the radar."

"I don't know if I can go along with this," said Archie. He was genuinely shocked.

"Then walk away, Archie," said Krystal. "Keep your distance, and just forget you were part of this conversation." She was beginning to regret her decision to bring Archie into the group.

Archie opened his mouth to speak but was interrupted by the buzz of his cell phone. He glanced at the screen and said, "Excuse me. I must take this call."

He listened for a moment, thanked the caller, and catching Krystal's eye said, "Lawrence Terrell attacked his psychiatrist and escaped from the clinic. They want me there."

Krystal was shocked. *What the hell else could happen?* "What are you going to do?"

"Make sure the Terrells are safe. Now that Lawrence has proven himself capable of violence, he may go after them. The psychiatrist is in the hospital with a traumatic head injury and might not make it."

He stood to leave, and Strachey asked, "What's your decision about what we're discussing here, Archie?"

The cop went silent for a beat before heading for the door. "I'll let you know."

And he was gone.

Whitehall was not pleased. "I don't like this. The man is a wild card, and I don't like wild cards. He must be brought back into the deck."

“How do we do that?” asked Krystal. “Archie has principles, and he’ll do what he thinks right.”

Whitehall did not respond, which in its own way was worrisome.

The gray man reached into his suit pocket and produced a cell phone which he handed to Strachey. “Use this phone and only this phone to contact me. The number is already in the phone. You may call me at any time of day or night. I will not be returning to Washington until we have this sorted out.”

Whitehall glanced around the room, raking them with his eyes. “Please keep me informed of any further development.” The way he said it made the ‘please’ entirely superfluous.

Strachey looked at the cellphone in his hand. It was a simple flip phone. Was it encrypted, or was it just a burner? No way he could tell.

It didn’t make any difference.

CHAPTER 26

Krystal needed to be alone for a while. She was upset and worried about Archie. She retreated to her office leaving Strachey and Watson to whisky and cigars. Would Whitehall really go to extreme lengths to prevent leaks about the Wakefield case? Her experience with Whitehall had taught her that he was a resourceful man who could be subtle or ruthlessly direct as the situation demanded. Despite their acquaintance, she could not claim to know the man well. He had enormous resources at his disposal and had played the *éminence grise* in the Washington swamp for decades. Literally, the man was capable of anything. If Archie refused to go along with his plan, what would be the consequence?

She had to convince Archie to play along.

And now the Terrell case had blown up in their faces. Strachey's insistence that they take the case because it was good business stuck in her craw. She had not been enthusiastic about having Terrell as a client from the start. Now, it was entirely possible that reports of their association with Lawrence Terrell would find their way into the press, and that definitely would not be good for business.

A half-hour later, her cell phone rang. She was surprised to see it was Archie calling. "I wanted to share this with you," he said, his voice grim.

"You found Lawrence?"

"No, he's still in the wind."

"What happened with the doctor?" she asked.

"That's what I wanted to tell you. The shrink was overconfident according to witnesses. Terrell grabbed a paperweight from his desk and smashed him in the head several times. The doctor was rushed to Carolinas Medical Center, and they're still working on him."

"What about the family?"

"They are terrified."

"With good reason. I think he'll go after them now. He truly hates them, you know."

"It's possible, but it's just as likely he will get as far away from Charlotte as he can. But he's crazy enough to do anything, and I'm putting a man at the Terrell house for the time being."

"That's a good idea. But keep in mind that logic is not a part of Lawrence's make-up. He wants revenge and is likely to go after Mary and Randolph, especially now that they tried to lock him up."

"I don't doubt that you're right."

"Thanks for calling, Archie. I do appreciate it." She paused a moment, uncertain what to say next. "Uh, Archie, we should meet and talk about the other thing."

"I know." He didn't sound happy, "but it'll have to wait until I get this thing handled."

She sat in her office in gloomy silence. She had acted professionally in the Terrell matter. She was doing her job, distasteful as it was. It was something expected of her. But she could not shake the nagging, completely illogical thought that she was somehow at fault. The Terrell family history was tragic, and it was rubbing off on her. She would never again allow herself to be pushed into doing something her instincts warned her against. Even if it might be good for business, it was not good for the soul.

Lawrence Terrell may have raped his twin sister and driven her to suicide. He was deranged and unpredictable, and she was certain of one thing. He would not be deterred from his quest to avenge his father's fate, however twisted his logic. He would try to get at Mary and Randolph, and a police car at the Terrell home might not be enough deter him.

CHAPTER 27

She returned to Strachey's office to fill them in on Terrell. Strachey was fiddling with another cigar, and there was a bottle of scotch and a bottle of bourbon on the coffee table between them. "Are you guys just drinking?"

Not for the first time, she wished she could join them.

Strachey scowled and gestured for her to take a seat.

"We need to get your buddy back on the team," said Watson.

Strachey raked her with a speculative eye. "Do you think you can convince him?"

"Frankly," she said, "I don't know. Archie is a stubborn guy, and he has principles. He also just got pulled in up to his elbows with the Terrell case, and he's worried about Captain Curry."

"Archie has gone out of his way to help you in the past," said Strachey, then added, "And he's sweet on you."

She felt herself reddening. "I don't know about that."

"Oh, yes, you do" continued Strachey, "the signs are unmistakable. He's been mooning around you for months. You must have noticed the way he looks at you."

Watson chimed in. "There's no mistaking those hound dog eyes. He's smitten. You're the mason jar to his preserves, for sure."

"You, too, Frank?" She was irritated, but she had to laugh at Frank. She knew they were right. She had not yet sorted out precisely how she felt about Archie. He was a great guy, and they saw eye to eye on most things.

"You've got to turn him around," said Strachey. "Our Russian may not be acting alone. He could have some help and a base of operations somewhere. We don't know how many people we're dealing with, and we need Archie."

The thought that the danger had not passed took her aback. "Three bad guys are already down, two of them dead. How many more could there be?"

Strachey shook his head. "I don't know. You're right. We may have all of them. But Archie still must be convinced to work with us."

"You mean manipulate him; take advantage of these feelings you say he has. I don't like manipulating people."

Strachey shrugged. "You're a woman, aren't you? I'm sure you can do it. And besides, you like him, too," he added through a sly grin.

Maybe she did, but it was none of Strachey's damn business. "I'll think about it," she said at last. "He just called me with more news about the Terrell thing."

"And?"

"Lawrence is still at large. Archie is posting a man at Mary and Randolph's house. I really feel bad about this, Bob."

"It's not your fault," replied Strachey.

His 'you're a woman, aren't you' had ignited a slow burn which now flared up. "We should never have accepted the job, and I hope you'll trust my gut in future, no matter how good it might seem for business."

Chastened, Strachey did not react to her accusatory tone. "OK, Krystal. You were right, and I was wrong. I accept the blame."

She had hoped for an argument to get her out of this conversation and had no rejoinder to his admission of guilt. It didn't make her feel any better.

"That being said," Strachey continued, "you still need to get to Archie and convince him hold his tongue."

"He's a good cop. Holding his tongue could cost him his job," she said.

"It could cost more," said Watson. "Your FBI friend could make him disappear into a dark cell somewhere in Mongolia."

Her voice tinged with bitterness, she said, "Whitehall has no business threatening us … or Archie."

"I agree," said Strachey. "He's a strange old bird, but he has his reasons, one of which is that he no longer trusts his own bureaucracy. Everything in Washington is political. And if you want to know what I think, he's afraid to bring more FBI people in because he can't predict what they might do. The old guard is no longer in control, and I'm frankly surprised that Whitehall hasn't been given the boot. Given the way things are in this administration, they will want to avoid any more scandal with an election coming up next year. They might even think it would have been more convenient if our Russian assassin had been successful and left the country quietly. A murder or two in faraway Charlotte would cause no ripples in the swamp water."

She was taken aback. "Jeez, Bob, you spent too much time in Washington. That sounds like you think the FBI might want to knock us off themselves."

"I did spend too much time in Washington," he said, "and things have only gotten worse since I left, at the FBI and the CIA, too." He did not try to contradict what she had said.

Watson had followed their conversation closely, not wanting to interfere, but now he spoke up. "What that means is that this thing better get finished PDQ 'cause from where I sit, we're lookin' at the south end of northbound dog." He squinted at Krystal. "You're gonna need your cop buddy, but I don't think you need me any longer now that the bad guy is in custody. I gotta get back to the wife and kids."

Krystal was genuinely sorry to see her old friend go. "We're going to miss you, Frank. I've gotten used to having you around again."

"Well, Red," he said, "I'm always just up the road a ways if you need me. But you have good ol' Archie here to comfort you." He laughed at his own joke.

She felt herself reddening. "One of these days, Frank, I'm going to slug you. And do you know what? I'll feel good about it."

Frank raised his arms in mock defense. "Aw, Red, you're hurtin' my feelings. I thought you loved me."

She surrendered. "Damnit, Frank Watson, I do. And I will miss you despite how evil you can be."

When he was gone, Strachey said, "I hate to nag, but what about Archie?"

Defeated, she said, "I'll call him, try to set up a meeting. But I don't think Whitehall has abduction and murder in mind, least of all against any of us."

"But," said Strachey, "he'll do whatever he must to make this thing disappear."

CHAPTER 28

Night had fallen, and it was raining again. Krystal and Archie sat in her living room. Archie wore a haggard look from a grueling day as well as the night before spent on guard outside Krystal's house and at the hospital. Exhausted, he sprawled in an easy chair and stretched his long legs while Krystal prepared a pot of coffee in the kitchen.

She returned to the living room with two thick porcelain navy mugs on a tray which she placed on a low table. "You look like shit, Archie."

He gave her a wan smile. "I guess I do. I've been dealing with Mary and Randolph Terrell all afternoon. Mary is nearly hysterical."

"I'm sorry." Poor Archie, she thought. He'd not slept in 48 hours.

"It's not your fault Lawrence came back to town."

"I feel like I stirred up a hornets' nest. We should never have taken his case."

"He would have found someone else."

"Is there any word on the injured shrink?"

"He had a fractured skull, but they think he'll pull through."

"Can he talk?"

"Not yet. They're keeping him sedated until the brain swelling goes down."

"We should talk about the other thing, Archie. We really need you on the team."

"The team? I'm still thinking about it. Curry wants to talk to me again tomorrow morning about the attempt on you."

"What are you going to tell him."

"I haven't decided yet."

"Archie, you can't tell him any more than we did this morning. Let the FBI take care of it."

He looked so mournful she almost wanted to hug him. "Krystal, the truth is, I don't know what to do."

"We need you, Archie. We can trust no one else."

Archie stirred restlessly. "This should be an official case with the police fully briefed. Robert Strachey is an old spook, so I can understand where he's coming from. But you? You were a cop. You know how this should be handled."

He was right from a cop's perspective, but she had seen things he had not. "While I was up in Arlington, I saw a lot of things you wouldn't believe, and a lot of it had to do with politics. There is a lot more here than meets the eye," she said, and explained Strachey's theory about FBI involvement.

Archie was incredulous. "He really believes that?"

"Yes, and Whitehall believes it, too. The FBI is not to be trusted, at least some elements in it. We're on our own, and so is Whitehall. He'll do whatever he thinks he must."

Archie closed his eyes and rested his head back on the chair, his coffee untouched. They spent a long moment in silence before it was interrupted by the chirp of Archie's mobile phone. He answered, and his face turned ashen as he listened. When he was finished, he stood. "I've got to go."

"What is it?" The alarm was evident on his face.

"Randolph Terrell has been murdered," he said. "And Lawrence is barricaded in a bedroom with his mother. I've got to get over there."

"I'm going with you." Her tone brooked no objection.

CHAPTER 29

Getting into the house was easy. After all, Lawrence had grown up here, spent 14 years playing in the yard and throughout the house. He knew where the shadows were between the security lights and the locations of all the doors. He had broken into houses before, but the set of keys he had permitted a silent entry through a back door. Passing through the kitchen, he selected a large butcher knife from the wooden block on the counter. He could hear his uncle and mother talking and tracked the sound to the study, his father's study.

His mother shrieked when she saw him, and his uncle stepped in front of her. Lawrence laughed as he moved in, the knife ready in his hand. His uncle attempted to grapple with him, but Lawrence was too strong and soon the knife found its mark several times, but not before his Randolph shouted at Mary to run and call the police.

Lawrence knew there was a policeman posted in front of the house and immediately pursued his mother, catching her before she could reach the door. But her scream had alerted the guard. He dragged

Mary up the stairs to the bedroom and barricaded the door..

It was a short drive to Myers Park where they found three police cruisers and an EMS van crowded in front of the house bathing it in a kaleidoscope of red and blue. A uniformed officer stepped towards the jeep. “He’s still holding the wife hostage in the bedroom upstairs, sir. Should we call SWAT?”

“No. We need finesse, not a blunt instrument. SWAT would just get everybody killed. What’s happening inside?” Archie’s weariness had dissipated to be replaced with crisp professionalism.

“We have two men stationed outside the bedroom door and two more outside watching the window. The medics are with the victim.”

Archie did a double take. “Randolph is still alive?”

“Barely.”

This was a welcome surprise, but Archie was angry. “How did Terrell get into the house?”

The officer was embarrassed. “It looks like he had a set of keys and got in through a back door. We thought the house was secure.”

Archie glared at the cop before turning to Krystal. “Are you sure you want to do this?”

“Lawrence knows me, Archie. Maybe I can talk him down.”

“Come on, then.”

The study was toward the back of the house. They found two medical technicians bent over a prone form on the floor while a police officer watched. There was a lot of blood.

“I thought he was dead.” Archie addressed one of the cops.

“Damn near,” said one of the medics over his shoulder. “He’s lost a lot of blood and has some serious internal injuries. We’re preparing him to be transported to the hospital. It will be touch and go for him.”

Archie grabbed Krystal’s elbow. “We’d better get upstairs.”

Two cops were stationed outside the bedroom door. Mary’s whimpering was audible from inside.

“Is he armed?” Archie asked.

“He only has a knife, as far as we know,” whispered one of the cops.

Archie turned to her. “Go ahead and give it a try,” he urged.

Her mouth suddenly dry, Krystal moved to the door. “Lawrence, it’s Krystal Murphy. Can we talk?”

Terrell’s voice was a rasping growl. “There’s no more to talk about. If you and the cops can’t give me justice, I’ll do it myself.”

“It’s not too late, Lawrence. The psychiatrist and Randolph are still alive. You aren’t a murderer. I’ve tried to help you, Lawrence. I’m the only person who has been on your side, and I still am. Please, let me in so we can talk.”

Terrell expelled a bitter laugh. “You already told me you have nothing. You’re working against me, too.”

“No, I’m not. I promise. Let me help you.”

“How can you help me?”

“Just let me come in there, and we can talk about it.”

“You’ll bring the cops in.”

“No, I promise. I’ll be alone. Then just you and I can figure this thing out,” she tried in her most sympathetic voice.

There was a long silence behind the door.

Archie whispered, “What do you think you can do once you’re in there?”

"I don't know, but at least we'll be inside the room."

A tinge of uncertainty colored Lawrence's voice. "No guns?"

"No guns. I don't want to hurt you. I'm on your side, remember?"

"I'll kill my mother if you try anything." Stress level rising.

"I know, Lawrence. You can trust me."

"Wait a second."

A muffled scream and a loud thud came from behind the door causing widened eyes and alarm among those outside. Before they could react, Lawrence said. "I'm clearing the door and unlocking it. Wait five seconds before you come in. And you had better be alone. If I see a uniform, my mother dies."

They could hear him moving something and then the click of the lock. Krystal drew her pistol from its holster and stuck it in her waist at the small of her back. She counted to five. "I'm coming in now, Lawrence."

She opened the door. Mary Terrell was sprawled on the floor, leaning back against Lawrence. She looked unconscious. Lawrence had struck her so he could leave her long enough to clear the door. He now knelt behind her body holding a knife to her throat.

Krystal lifted her jacket away from her body so he could see the empty holster. “No gun,” she said.

Mary was beginning to stir.

“I wanted you to see this,” grinned Lawrence, his voice now calm. “You did nothing to help me, but you can witness my justice.”

He bent to his mother, the edge of the knife at her throat as a trickle of blood appeared.

There was no choice. Krystal reached behind her back, drew out the pistol and fired. The 40-caliber slug struck Lawrence in the arm, throwing him back and away from Mary. The knife flew from his grip. He howled with pain. “You promised!”

Archie and the two cops rushed into the room and subdued Lawrence before he could rise. Krystal knelt beside Mary. The wound to her neck was superficial. Lawrence had not had time to draw the knife across her throat.

She helped Mary to a chair as the cops led a manacled and bleeding Lawrence from the room still howling with a mixture of rage and pain.

“Archie, get one of the medics up here.”

CHAPTER 30

It was nearly 2:30 A.M., and Dean Robbins wished he were home in bed instead of sitting in an uncomfortable chair outside a hospital room. The man lying in the bed inside the room was the prime suspect in a shooting the evening before. He was in bad shape and unlikely to try to escape, but Sergeant Archie Wolf wanted the room to be guarded, and Officer Robbins drew the short straw. He loved being a cop on the street but hated this kind of assignment, and he disliked hospitals even more.

He stifled a yawn and returned to the book he was reading, an old Zane Grey novel. At 2:00 A.M. The hospital was quiet with only the nurses making their routine rounds.

A blond man in hospital scrubs approached down the corridor. "How is it going, Officer?" he asked. He spoke with an accent Robbins did not recognize.

Robbins looked up from his novel. "Boring," he replied.

The man held out a tall paper cup with a plastic lid. "I thought you might like some coffee," he said with a smile. "These nights can get pretty long. "I brought it up from the cafeteria."

"Gosh, thanks," said Robbins. "That would hit the spot, all right."

He accepted the cup.

"Well," said the man, "have a good night. I must make my rounds now." And he strolled away down the corridor.

Robbins popped the plastic lid off the cup. It was a latte. It was hot, and it smelled good. He took a tentative sip and sighed in appreciation. It only took ten minutes to finish it, and he set the cup on the floor beside his chair.

He turned back to his novel, but a lethargy began to take hold of him, and within minutes he slumped in the chair in a deep sleep.

*****

The twin emotions of frustration and rage tore at Yuriy Volodin's guts. He lay shackled to a bed, his head clouded by drugs, and weak from blood loss. He assessed his chances of escape under such conditions as nil.

Failure had dogged this mission. Tasks that seemed at a distance to be simple had proven difficult. Worse, thanks to the disaster in Georgia, he had lost two team members, both good men. And now yet another failure. The auburn-haired woman should have been eliminated on his first try, but somehow, she had escaped, and worse, had fired back at him with military precision. Volodin was not accustomed to his targets returning fire. His forté was the ambush; one clean shot or a sudden attack on an unprepared target.

Everything had gone off the rails.

An opportunity had presented itself, but again, fate had intervened to save his would-be victim.

If he could not complete his mission, returning to Moscow would be a dicey proposition, presuming even that some sort of prisoner trade could be arranged. Explanations that the targets were tougher than expected, that the environment was difficult and unfamiliar, none of this would suffice. Logic and operational security did not matter where the president was concerned, and Klichkov would bend to the president's will every time.

Volodin was an expert with a long gun. He had dispatched Wakefield from well over 1,000 feet from the cover of dense woods. But within the crowded confines of an urban environment, the logistics were different and more difficult. Spaces were more enclosed, and cover was scarce.

And now his situation had become untenable. He was in police custody and too weak to escape, his thoughts meandered in a drug-induced fugue to such an extent that he even considered doing a deal with the Americans. Surely he had information they would find interesting.

A male nurse in hospital scrubs came into the room. He did something at the rack of transfusion bags at the side of the bed and then left. The weariness and hopelessness of his situation overcome Volodin. Would he end his days in some dank cell in an American prison.

CHAPTER 31

Hospital waiting rooms are never pleasant places, especially surgical waiting rooms where relatives and friends fret awaiting the results of procedures. The atmosphere is filled with tension punctuated with occasional sobs and quick intakes of breath. The surgical waiting room of Atrium Health Carolinas is no exception.

Krystal and Archie sat with Mary Terrell. Lawrence's knife had not caused her significant injury and she required only a simple dressing on her neck. The hands on the wall clock were passing midnight, and Randolph had been in the operating room for over two hours.

Captain Curry had made an appearance shortly after their arrival and was displeased to see Krystal there with Archie. Before leaving, he made it clear that he expected to see her in his office the following day.

Ironically, all three victims in the Terrell case were being treated in the same hospital. Dr. Dudek was slowly recovering from Lawrence's attack in intensive care, Randolph Terrell was undergoing surgery in one operating theater while Lawrence was being treated in another. Of the three, Randolph was the most serious. He had lost a lot of blood before the medics arrived. The surgeon had made no promises.

Archie informed Krystal that her would-be killer was in a guarded room on another floor.

Mary was in a state of sustained shock. "My God," she mumbled, "what have we done?" She leaned forward and put her face in her hands. "We made so many mistakes."

Krystal's presentiment that the Terrell case was one to avoid confirmed her belief that it was best to trust one's gut. But regardless of her aversion, the clues she had uncovered intrigued her. What really happened that night when Lawrence's twin sister had drowned? Had Lawrence been responsible for her death? And what about James Terrell who had disappeared without a trace? Mary was the key which could unlock everything. The question was whether she would be willing to talk, given everything that had transpired.

It was nearly dawn before the surgeon reappeared, his gown splattered with blood, his face haggard. As he approached, they all rose to their feet.

He stopped in front of Mary and solemnly took her hands in his. "Your husband was very gravely injured, Mrs. Terrell. It was a close thing, and he lost a great deal of blood, but with some time and the grace of God, I think he has a fighting chance. We'll have to wait and see, but I am cautiously optimistic."

Mary nearly collapsed in his arms, and he eased her back into a chair. "May I see him?" she quavered.

"Not just yet. He'll be in recovery for some time as we monitor his vital signs. He will be moved to a room in ICU for the time being." Casting a glance at Krystal and the others, he continued, "I think it would be best for your friends to take you home now so you can get some rest. You've had a rough time, and you need to look after yourself now. You can see your husband later in the morning."

Reluctantly, Mary accompanied Krystal to the exit while Archie retrieved his jeep and drove around to pick them up. Mary recoiled a little at the appearance of the perpetually muddy jeep.

The woman was in a fragile state, and Krystal would have to play it by ear. Mary might collapse from stress and shock. But if treated gently and with sympathy, she might open up. Unwillingly or not, Krystal had been drawn into this family tragedy and felt an unreasonable guilt for what had happened. She knew she bore no responsibility for Lawrence's actions, but she had become part of the entire sordid mess, nevertheless.

CHAPTER 32

Strachey stretched out on the sofa in his office at PSI. After sending his family away, he had locked up the family home and activated the security system which he could monitor remotely from the office. He had considered posting PSI contractors at the house but concluded that it would be unfair to place them in the line of fire without knowing what was really going on. In the meantime, the office was comfortable. He had a private bathroom and shower *en suite* with his office, as well as several changes of clothes. He looked forward to life returning to normal.

The immediacy of the threat to himself, his family, and his friends had dissipated, but he could not fall asleep. He finally gave up at 4:00 A.M. He showered, skipped shaving, and dressed in jeans and a light cotton pullover sweater.

The steam punk coffee machine on the bar was a source of constant delight. The time he had spent in Spain had addicted him to the kind of strong, black coffee they served there, and he set about making a *café negro doble* to which he added two cubes of brown raw sugar.

Coffee in hand, he opened his humidor and selected an Oliva Seria V 135 Aniversario perfecto. Cigars were not a habit for Strachey; they were a choice and an avocation which made him as knowledgeable of tobacco and cigar vitolas as an oenophile was of wine. They also concentrated his thinking wonderfully, an essential aid to his process of reflection.

He became accustomed to real Habanos during his tour in Madrid where he spent many enjoyable afternoons with Spanish police buddies. Following long lunches which typically began at 2:00 P.M and ended not earlier than 5:00, the restaurant owner would set a box of Habanos on the table along with a bottle of scotch whisky, a bucket of ice, and tall glasses, all of which conspired to add another hour to the lunch routine. Brotherhood and camaraderie – that's what cigars and whisky engender.

Unfortunately, his friends in Spain now informed him that the non-smoking mania had hit there, as well. Back in the day, when manly pleasures were still condoned there, he was fond of saying that Spain was "the last Christian country in the world," *el ultimo país Cristiano en el mundo.* He lamented the loss of a more congenial past. Hell's bells, he thought, am I so old that I've become nostalgic for the past like some elderly resident of a nursing home? No, he decided, it was just that as time marched on, the world steadily lost its charm with no counterbalancing improvement.

Strachey missed his days in the CIA, and especially his years in Spain. He had saved Europe from a nuclear holocaust and been part of a team which took out a dangerous Russian dictator. With his trajectory on the rise, his decision to leave the Agency, therefore, had puzzled many, but his victories came at a price, and he had done something which made it impossible for him to remain with the Agency. He had killed a man. It was nothing he was ashamed of, but not something the Agency could condone.

He could still buy Habanos from a company in Switzerland, but he was growing weary of the spiraling prices. Only oil sheiks could afford the *crème de la crème* of Havana production these days at a thousand bucks a stick. He also found that today's Habanos were lacking the personality of the ones he had enjoyed in the 90's. So, he was turning increasingly to an improved range of non-Cuban cigars and was especially fond of tobaccos from Nicaragua. The cigar he chose this morning featured an Ecuadorian wrapper and Nicaraguan filler. The combination of strong coffee and nicotine would aid his concentration and soothe his nerves.

He should call Enoch Whitehall to see how his plan, whatever it was, was progressing. But it was far too early. Whatever the plan was, Whitehall would have to move fast.

Strachey had never had a good relationship with the FBI. As a CIA operative he had viewed the Legal Attachés – FBI agents assigned to embassies – as supercilious pricks. The Bureau was obsessed with evidence that could stand up in a court of law. That was fine, but in an operational context, as the CIA saw it, results were more important than tying up a legal case with a pretty bow.

He had to admit, however, that Enoch Whitehall was an anomaly. As the FBI's Executive Assistant Director for Counterintelligence, he wielded considerable authority. But Whitehall had not demonstrated a great deal of concern for form and legality. There was a lot of politics in what the quintessentially gray man did, the arcane, backstreet knife fights of Washington, and his recent pronouncements about the Russian assassins certainly had nothing to do with the law and everything to do with expediency. Of late, politics had certainly dominated over the law in Washington, DC. Whitehall's insistence on keeping this matter out of official channels reflected the way the current was flowing in today's swamp water. Strachey suspected the captive Russian would disappear into a federal facility never to be heard from again. He had no problem with that.

His coffee cup was empty, and he returned to the bar to brew another. He carried the coffee back to the sofa, sat down, and stretched his legs out on the coffee table. It would be at least another hour or more before sunrise, and he would use the time to think. The strong, thick coffee was gone after a few sips, and he settled back with what remained of his cigar. The only light in the office came from his desk lamp, and it was dead quiet, the perfect atmosphere for contemplation. Something was wrong. But what was it?

Despite her own narrow escape, Krystal was consumed by the Terrell case about which she felt unaccountably guilty. The events of a decade ago and their consequences could in no way be attributed to anything Krystal Murphy had done. But she had a powerful sense of responsibility layered over a streak of stubbornness. These attributes were what had attracted Strachey to her in the first place and convinced him to recruit her. And she had proven to be a star who would doggedly pursue difficult cases to the bitter end.

Her personal life was another thing entirely. She was a private person, and that led to keeping things to herself that might best be shared with a friend. Krystal had had to fight her way up the ladder from humble origins, through the military, and up the ranks of the Arlington Police. She had successfully fought misogyny and shown that she was the equal of any man. But all this had put a chip on her shoulder which could be troublesome, sometimes getting in the way of good decisions. Regardless, Strachey did not for a moment regret having her on his team.

Krystal had gone through a rough patch the year before and retreated into a bottle of scotch, and this had worried her friends mightily. People like Krystal had a hard time trusting others. When they finally did and were then betrayed, they fell hard. That's what had happened to her. Strachey and his wife, Amy, had been determined to see her through that rough patch.

His thoughts were straying. Whatever nagged at his subconscious, it wasn't Krystal Murphy's love life. But maybe it had something to do with her. That's the way the subconscious works.

CHAPTER 33

The rain had slackened when Krystal accompanied Mary into the empty house while Archie remained outside. "Is there anything I can get you?" she asked, "Anything I can do for you?"

Mary Terrell just kept walking without responding, her gait stiff, and Krystal followed her into a room at the back of the house which boasted a small bar.

"I need a drink," said Mary. She grabbed a bottle of bourbon from the bar and splashed a generous amount into a glass. She sat and promptly downed half of the strong whiskey. Leaning her head against the back of the chair, she sighed. "We should have put him away for good ten years ago," she said to the air, and then downed the rest of her drink.

Krystal assumed she was speaking of Lawrence.

Holding the empty glass out to Krystal, Mary said, "Please refill it for me, and don't be stingy."

Krystal hesitated. "Are you sure? Shouldn't you try to get some rest now? You'll have a busy day tomorrow."

Mary gave her a baleful stare. "Rest? You think I can rest after all this?" She waved an arm in a vague, all-encompassing gesture. Pour me another or I'll do it myself."

Krystal obliged. The night's tragedy had transformed Mary from the uncertain, timid woman she had met only a few days ago into something else entirely. The shock was wearing off with the aid of alcohol to be replaced by a kind of resignation.

"Do you want to talk about it?" Krystal handed the recharged glass to Mary who promptly knocked back another mouthful.

She looked up at Krystal and shrugged. "Why the hell not? What do you want to know?"

Krystal sat on the edge of a chair facing Mary. "Maybe we should start at the beginning, ten years ago."

Mary stared at her bourbon. "Oh, it started long before that. It was James, you see. He ... he changed over the years. Oh, he always had a roving eye. He swept me away because I thought he was exciting to be with. And, of course, he came from a good family."

Krystal interpreted the word "good" to connote wealth. She obliged Mary's request and poured her yet another bourbon, careful this time to provide a shorter measure. Mary didn't seem to notice.

"But after the children were born, he just couldn't help himself around other women, especially younger women. Maybe it was me. I put on some weight during the pregnancy and had some trouble getting rid of it. I had twins, after all. And he liked younger women, you see. The younger the better.

"At first, I resented it, but there were the children, and I wanted to preserve the marriage. I decided there was no changing him. Randolph saw what was happening, but he could not persuade James to change his ways. It was then that Randolph and I became close. His wife had died, you see, and I had comforted him in his grief. But now it was my turn to cry on his shoulder." She shot a fierce look at Krystal. "But there was nothing illicit between us. I kept my wedding vows even if James did not."

Mary held the empty whiskey glass in her slightly trembling hand, a faraway look in her eyes as she stared into the past. Tears came now, but her voice remained steady as they rolled down her cheek. "It got worse the older the children grew."

She was whispering now. "Fannie was such a lovely young girl, and Lawrence idolized his sister. But as she blossomed into womanhood, James became fixated on her. He would burst into her room as she was dressing and hold her too tightly when he hugged her. His attention became obsessive. Fannie became afraid of him and tried to avoid him, but he was persistent. Then came that night ..." She went silent for a few beats, the tears streaming now as the memory returned.

"I should have done something sooner, but I felt helpless." A sob escaped her, a deep, visceral sob which wracked her body. She dropped the empty glass on the floor and bent, head in her hands. "I hate it that I was so weak."

Krystal waited for the moment to pass. She did not want to do anything to deter Mary from her story. She was at the point where she would either shut down altogether or continue speaking. Eventually, Mary seemed to recover.

Krystal held her breath.

"That night ..." Mary continued. "We had all retired for the evening, and I was asleep. At some point, James must have gone into Fannie's room and ..." Her voice broke again before she shuddered and continued. "Some time must have passed before we were awakened by Lawrence's shout from outside. James had come back to bed, and we both rushed downstairs. Lawrence was kneeling over his sister's body trying to revive her, but it was hopeless by then, and he was hysterical. You see, she had carried two heavy stones into the pool and managed to hold onto them until she lost consciousness. I couldn't understand why Fannie was naked or why she had done what she did. But Lawrence knew. Fannie had written a note and slipped it under his door before going down to the pool. Something must have awakened Lawrence, maybe it was his sister's passing – they were twins, after all – but by the time he reached her, it was already too late.

"Lawrence was inconsolable. He wept hysterically, and I think something must have broken inside him. He was only 14, and his sister's death changed him forever. Later, after the police had been there and Fannie's body had been taken away, Lawrence showed me Fannie's note. Her father had raped her and promised to do it again because, he told her, she should like it now that she was a woman."

Mary's face twisted in disgust. "Can you imagine it. 14 years old! I told James he would have to leave because I would report him to the police. I had Fannie's note. I don't know if he was ashamed of what he had done, but he seemed to feel some guilt, maybe even shame, if he were capable of such a thing. He was certainly shocked at what Fannie had done. He agreed to leave, begged me to give him enough time to disappear before calling the police."

"Lawrence must have overheard our conversation. When James went into his study, I suppose to collect documents and car keys, Lawrence followed him. He had taken a hammer from the garage, and he walked up behind his father and smashed the hammer into his head. I think James must have died instantly. That's how I found them, Lawrence standing over his father's body holding the hammer. He wouldn't say a word.

"I could think of nothing to do but call Randolph. I think Randolph must have loved me since we were in college. He came over immediately and took charge. I was in such a state that I could barely speak. We were both worried for Lawrence. We could not permit him to be arrested, least of all because of what James had done, so we decided that the only way to protect him would be to dispose of James's corpse and say he had disappeared. We knew there would be consequences, but our only thought was to protect Lawrence. We knew he needed help, but not at the hands of the authorities."

And there it was. The entire mystery of James Terrell's disappearance cleared up in a few moments. It was a lot to take in, more than Krystal could have hoped for. And it gave her a different perspective on Lawrence. He was both perpetrator and victim. Was it possible that she could feel some sympathy for him now?

"What did you do with James's body?" she asked. Krystal had gotten this far, and she wanted all the answers now no matter how brutal the question.

"Oh," replied Mary, "Randolph put him on his boat at Nags Head. He returned a few days later and took him out to sea where he dropped the body."

"What about Dr. Dudek?"

"He was probably a mistake." Mary shook her head. "Dr. Dudek was well respected in our community, and he knew how to keep a secret. We told him we wanted to make sure that Lawrence did not remember what he had done. We really didn't want him to remember any of the horror. Dudek agreed to accept the task. I think he found it intellectually stimulating. We thought that if the memory of killing his father and why he had done it could be erased, Lawrence might have a chance at a normal life. After a year of treatment, Dudek pronounced Lawrence 'cured,' and released him from care. We thought it best to send him away from Charlotte and all the rumors and gossip about his father's disappearance and chose a nice school in New England. He disappeared after only a week up there, and we didn't see him again until he showed up here."

There it was. The entire story. Krystal could think of nothing to say.

Mary turned to her. "So, now you know. I can't go on any longer with this morbid charade. Nothing you do now could be any worse."

CHAPTER 34

Krystal stepped outside to inform Archie that she would remain with Mary throughout the night until she was on an even keel and could return to the hospital. She told him he should go home for some long overdue rest and pick them up in the morning to take Mary back to the hospital. Archie insisted on remaining there. He would catch some sleep in his jeep, he said.

She urged Mary to at least try to get some rest and assured her that she would be there if needed, then settled down on a sofa in the living room. She had not mentioned a word of Mary's confession to Archie. She had not intended it so, but she felt somehow constrained.

After over a decade, the mystery of James Terrell's disappearance was solved, and apart from the principals, Krystal Murphy was the only person to know the truth. Even Lawrence did not know the truth.

Now, she wasn't sure what she should do with this truth, which was much different from earlier speculation. All the Terrells were victims, beginning with

Fannie and ending with Lawrence. Mary's revelations, whether elicited by shock or conscience, were shot through with such torment and grief, such hopelessness and surrender that the effect dampened any satisfaction Krystal may have felt.

This house, she reflected, was a venue of tragedy haunted by the phantoms of unspeakable acts and death. The memories, the guilt, the sorrow must have weighed heavily on its remaining inhabitants, hounding them like an evil spirit. But they were anchored in the place, trapped their collective knowledge of what had happened and their collective guilt in covering it up.

Was it family pride which had driven them to such extremes or love for a son who was destined to hate them? They had tried to shield Lawrence from knowledge of his patricide but subjecting him to whatever treatments Dr. Dudek had devised did more harm than good. The resulting imperfect and twisted memories brought Lawrence back to wreak vengeance on the very people who had tried to protect him.

What would happen now? Lawrence was guilty of murdering his father, as well as attacks on Dudek and Randolph

Terrell. Mary and Randolph were guilty of concealing James's murder and disposing of his body. The entire, dysfunctional clan had transgressed the law. But what punishment could be worse than what they had imposed upon themselves already?

These thoughts were interrupted by Mary who came downstairs fully dressed and insisted on returning to the hospital.

*****

Krystal had managed what seemed only a few moments' sleep at the Terrell house and felt tired to the bone. Having deposited Mary at the hospital, she and Archie drove to Krystal's townhouse, and she invited Archie, who by now was completely enervated, to try to get some rest on the living room sofa. They had to talk about Whitehall's demands, but neither of them was in a fit condition to do so right now. By then, it was a quarter past five.

She went upstairs, stripped, and took a long, hot shower and turned off her cell phone before setting the alarm for 11:00 A.M. and falling into bed, hoping for a few hours' sleep, but Mary's confession and the decision she must make about it kept her awake despite the fatigue.

Downstairs Archie stretched out on the sofa, his legs dangling over the arm. He had removed his holster and service pistol and laid them on the floor next to his shoes. He felt as though he had just fallen asleep when he was awakened by a loud knock on the door.

Whoever it was called out, "Police."

Still groggy, he checked his watch and saw that it was just after 6 A.M. *What the hell had happened now,* he wondered. *Had Randolph Terrell died?*

Mumbling curses under his breath, he padded in stocking feet to the door.

When he opened it, a bullet tore through his chest, knocking him to the floor. Another round slammed into the floor beside his head as the shooter walked past.

CHAPTER 35

Strachey realized he was hungry. There was a small but efficient kitchen just down the hall where he rummaged in the refrigerator to see what he could turn up. It would be potluck, of course. He should have brought some food from home where an entire ham rested in the fridge.

Fortunately, he found a carton of eggs, a loaf of bread and some baloney. There was also half of an apple pie, from which he sliced a generous wedge. In short order, he carried a tray with his breakfast back to his office and twisted the brass knobs on his coffee machine to produce American-style coffee which he collected in a heavy porcelain cup.

The hands of Strachey's venerable but still reliable Rolex told him it was 5:00 A.M. He finished his breakfast and returned the plate and cutlery to the kitchen. He thought of calling Whitehall. The FBI man had shunted them aside when he assumed control of the supposed Russian, but Strachey felt he had a right to know what would happen to the man who had tried to kill his partner.

He hadn't bothered to examine the mobile phone Whitehall had given him before now. He had simply laid it on his desk after Whitehall departed. He picked it up now. One of the buttons on the keypad was red, suggesting it was a speed dial. He almost pressed the call button. Perhaps Whitehall really didn't sleep at all. Maybe he lay down each night fully dressed in his gray suit in a gray coffin. Or he just dematerialized. He decided not to call and replaced the phone on his desk.

There had been no word from Krystal since last night. The Terrells were murdering one another again. Krystal had said she would probably be at the hospital all night.

He needed more coffee, and not the American kind. He decided he also needed another cigar to aid digestion and help him think. He was jittery. Either from lack of sleep or an abundance of coffee, he had a bad feeling. It was a recidivist reaction, an instinctual return to his former life and the defensive reactions it entailed.

Old spooks always revert to type. The rules are inviolable. Always sit with your back to the wall facing the door. Always check your surroundings for anomalies. Never assume you are not under surveillance. Never, ever trust a first impression - as Reagan said, trust but verify. And sometimes, after years of experience, learn to trust your gut.

It can be hard to get to know a spook because they are always assessing you for recruitment potential. Even in retirement, they want to know what makes you tick, what you do, what you know, who you know, and the scrutiny can be discomfiting at times unless the spook is clever. Spook facades can be remarkably effective at disarming people. They can appear to be open and friendly, generous, charming - just a nice guy or gal who would like to be your friend.

Normal people may be forgiven for thinking that retired spooks should be happy to leave the old rules behind, forget all the intrigue, and enjoy life like anyone else. But that doesn't happen because the spook remembers the brushes with death and the large population of bad guys who might still be waiting to exact revenge.

His thoughts were interrupted by the buzz of a cell phone, the one Whitehall had given him. The FBI man had no qualms about calling at odd hours.

"Mr. Strachey," Whitehall's voice conveyed a sense of urgency which put Strachey immediately on guard. "Our prisoner is dead. I am convinced he was murdered. The man guarding the room was found unconscious a short while ago. When he regained consciousness, he said a man in hospital scrubs had given him a cup of coffee, and he remembered nothing after that. I'm sure you can surmise what that means."

Strachey sat perfectly still as the realization hit him of what had been nagging at the back of his brain. "There is another one," he said.

"Correct," replied Whitehall. "I've tried calling Ms. Murphy, but there is no answer. Perhaps she has turned her phone off. She and her policeman friend dropped off Mrs. Terrell and left the hospital some time ago. She should be warned."

"I'm on it," said Strachey. "I'll call you back."

He pulled out the large, lower drawer on the right side of his desk. It contained a safe to which only he knew the combination. It wasn't a modern, electronic safe with a keypad. It was an old fashioned safe with a tumbler mechanism. He twirled the dial in the proper sequence and lifted the heavy hatch. Inside, among other trophies of his past was a shoulder holster. It held a

Staccato C2 DPO 9mm semiautomatic pistol. He hefted its reassuring weight.

He ejected the mag and the chambered round and worked the slide. At somewhat over $2,000, the Staccato was not a cheap choice, but it was highly reliable and accurate. These days he could afford the best. The Staccato's handsome contours fit comfortably in his hand. A lot of people preferred larger calibers than the 9 mm, but Strachey chose his ammunition carefully for the damage it could do to a target. He had been hunting rabbits since he was nine, and he was a deadly accurate shot.

He reinserted the mag, pulled the slide back to load a round in the chamber, replaced the pistol in the holster, and slipped the rig around his shoulders. It required seven minutes to rush from his office to the parking garage.

Once on his way, he called Krystal but got no answer. At this time of the morning, it would take no more than ten minutes to reach her townhouse.

CHAPTER 36

Strachey skidded to a halt in front of the townhouse and was alarmed to see the front door standing open. Drawing his pistol, he rushed inside and nearly tripped over the body sprawled on the floor just inside.

Simultaneously, the pop-pop retort of a silenced pistol echoed from the direction of the stairs. Strachey sprinted toward the foot of the staircase. Illuminated against the light from the landing he saw a blond man dressed in dark trousers and sweatshirt half-way up the stairs pointing a pistol with the tell-tale extension of a silencer. He was firing through the wall at the corner of the landing, counting on his bullets piercing the hollow plasterboard to strike whoever was around the corner.

Strachey reacted swiftly, firing two shots. The man collapsed heavily and slid down the stairs.

Gasping for breath, he called out, "Krystal, are you OK? The guy is down and won't be getting back up."

Krystal appeared from around the corner at the top of the stairs. She wore a T-shirt and men's boxers and held her

Walther gripped tightly in her hand. Her eyes widened, and she raised the gun.

"Wait," shouted Strachey, "it's me!"

But she still fired. The rounds tore past Strachey who ducked instinctively as she fired again. "Krystal! Stop! It's me, Bob."

She relaxed, dropping her gun hand to her side. "I know," she said, "I was shooting at the guy behind you."

Strachey looked over his shoulder and saw another dark-clad man lying on his back at the foot of the stairs. "Jeez," he said, "there were two of them."

"Where is Archie?" she asked urgently.

Strachey's mind raced back to the body at the door. "Crap, Red, he's down. It looks bad." He turned and rushed back to the entrance with Krystal close behind.

Archie lay on his side leaking blood onto Krystal's beige wall-to-wall carpet. "Oh, my God," she cried. "Is he alive?"

Strachey knelt beside Archie, feeling for a pulse. "I think so, but he's unconscious and badly hurt. Call an ambulance while I try to stop the bleeding."

He darted to the kitchen and grabbed a towel to press over the wound. Archie had caught the slug in the chest, perilously close to his heart. With the lights now turned on, Strachey could see he was white as a sheet, and his lips were turning blue.

Krystal sat beside him and lifted his head into her lap. Tears ran down her cheeks and a sob escaped her. “Oh, Archie, just hang on. You can’t leave now.”

CHAPTER 37

It was ten in the morning, and for a change it wasn't raining. Archie had survived the trip in the ambulance to the hospital and was still in surgery. In response to a call from Whitehall, Strachey returned to the office, leaving an unusually fragile Krystal to await the results of the surgery. He felt bad about leaving her, but Enoch Whitehall called for a meeting.

The gray man sat facing Strachey. This morning, even he betrayed signs of weariness and had accepted a cup of strong coffee.

"Killing the man in the hospital was a display of typical Russian ruthlessness," he said. "They could not run the risk that he would talk. How they knew how to find him is a mystery we might never solve. In their own way, they can be efficient. But in doing so, they alerted us that the danger had not passed."

Strachey rubbed his eyes. "It was a close-run thing. Something was bothering me, and I finally realized what it was, although it was nearly too late. We had even speculated earlier that there may be more of them. We knew there were at least two others involved in the attack on Frank Watson, and in retrospect there was no reason to think there would not be more. There had to be someone here in Charlotte to research Krystal and me and lay the groundwork. As it turned out, there were two of them."

Whitehall agreed. "This is a mess," he said. "But I think we can still handle it. The dead man in the hospital is no longer a problem. He will simply disappear. But the fracas this morning is another matter entirely. There are too many witnesses, and the police are involved, especially given the involvement of Sergeant Wolf. Fortunately, they are treating the matter as a home invasion by assailants unknown. The two deceased intruders carried no identification, and I am not about to tell anybody that they were professional Russian assassins. In that sense, our problem has solved itself, with assistance from your friends – all the Russians are dead and unidentified. We will make certain there is no further investigation into their origins."

Whitehall's logic was sound, and he had the wherewithal to keep things from going off the rails. There was no point in opposing him. He also promised that he would find a way to express official displeasure to the Russians for sending a five-man assassination squad to the United States. A few key Russian diplomats would be quietly declared *persona non grata* and expelled from the country. Moreover, the pressure on Archie Wolf to cooperate unwillingly in an FBI cover-up was no longer necessary ... if Archie survived his injury.

"You'll have no argument from us, Director," said Strachey. "I only wish we could do more to the Russians than rap their knuckles."

The trace of a smile may have hovered around the gray man's lips. "Leave that to me, Mr. Strachey.

CHAPTER 38

She was at the hospital again. It had been an excruciatingly long morning as Archie lay on an operating table surrounded by surgeons and nurses. She felt helpless as hour piled upon hour.

It had been a year of privation, not only of abstinence from alcohol, but also from the warmth of human companionship. Krystal had friends, primarily the Stracheys, and family, but not the intimacy of the relationship of a man and woman. This had not bothered her so much during her younger years, her time in the military and later clawing her way through the ranks of the Arlington police. She had always been independent and career oriented. There had been the occasional man, of course, but nothing she took seriously.

It had not been until she met Ray Velazquez in Miami that a lacuna in her life she had not theretofore noticed had been filled. She experienced a sense of unexpected fulfillment, and the break-up had been shattering, even more so because she had only herself to blame. Ray had been willing to make the commitment, but she had not. She realized now that her fatal mistake had been to take Ray's affection for granted. She had grown so comfortable with the knowledge that he would always be there that she had not taken the warning signs seriously. Ray had had expectations, and rightly so, that she in her arrogance had ignored.

She was lonely.

Captain Abel Curry had been there with her since learning that Archie had been wounded, sitting in silence beside her, wrapped in his own thoughts.

At last, the surgeon appeared to inform them that although the surgery had been successful, the bullet had come dangerously close to Archie's heart which presented some complications. Archie remained in serious but stable condition, but recovery would be touch and go.

Curry thanked the doctor and turned to her. "He's going to need a friend to help him pull through this, Krystal."

"I know," she said.

He squeezed her arm and left after securing her promise to keep him informed.

Krystal was permitted into the ICU where she now sat next to Archie's bed holding his hand. The thought of losing him was crushing. She had not prayed in a long time, but she prayed now.

As for the Terrells, she had decided to tell no one what Mary had told her. She would leave it to Mary and Randolph whether to reveal the long-hidden truth of the disappearance of James Terrell.

There had been enough suffering and death for today.

THE END

Acknowledgements

A special thanks is due to my high-school classmate and loyal friend Judy Williams, inveterate world traveler and astute proofreader. My old colleagues and buddies Bob Hammond and Enrique Perez also deserve credit for encouraging me and reading the raw manuscript. Their corrections and suggestions were invaluable and very much appreciated. My cigar smoking buddy and minister John "Doc" Sloop played a part here also amidst a busy preaching schedule.

www.ingramcontent.com/pod-product-compliance
Lightning Source LLC
LaVergne TN
LVHW090601110826
845146LV00001B/211

* 9 7 9 8 2 1 8 4 3 3 0 8 6 *